My *Wedding* Date

My *Wedding* Date

Edited by Muneca Fossette

Stories by:

Carien Jordaan | Bevanny Stearman |
Rebecca Grace | Kelly Fauth | Jay Mendell |
Mimi Francis | Devon Borkowski | Penny Myles

4 Horsemen
Publications, Inc.

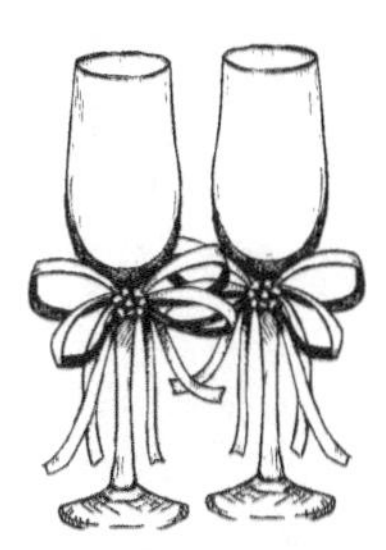

Table of Contents

Introduction

WHENEVER SOMEONE ANNOUNCES THAT they are getting married, they become recipients of unsolicited advice. Clichéd aphorisms like *"The key to a good marriage is trust/honesty/communication"* and *"Never go to bed angry"* slowly outnumber the items on the wedding registry. But that is the experience of those getting married. What about advice to wedding guests? Now, that is an untapped market. Therefore, with the help of this anthology's eight authors, I will now graciously offer wedding guests unsolicited advice. You're welcome in advance.

CHARGED ENCOUNTERS

- If you meet a hook-up prospect, do a quick background check. Who knows what concealed truths might lurk behind that gorgeous stranger at the wedding reception? Cue another cliché: Sometimes the truth is creepier than fiction. ("Petunias and Parenting at a Wedding")

- New (read: barely started dating/smashing/or other verbing) romantic interests do not make the best Plus Ones. Invite them at your peril. You might find yourself alone, stumbling through an intoxicating cocktail of mushrooms and reminiscences in a sex- and comma-filled satirical homage to masculine tropes ("Rocketship Derivative")

- Expect the unexpectedly expected and expectedly unexpected. You will run into an ex-lover or ex-friend at the wedding. Bank on it. But you might run into a known stranger who entices you into a life of simulated crime ("Stealing Cake").

- Never assume that you are the only assassin invited to a wedding. Sometimes killers love. And sometimes lovers (or their family members) kill. ("Til Death Do Us Part")

RESUMED ENCOUNTERS

- Sharing a hotel room with an ex is a bad idea. Or is it a good idea? I'll leave that up to you ("Complimentary Breakfast")

- Bring an extra set of clothes and shoes with you. You never know when something will break or when you will have to break someone the hell out of a wedding reception ("Could be Worse")

- If you don't remember a person, is your exchange a reunion? No, that's not advice. I'm asking. Anyway ... Sometimes reunions lead to love. Sometimes they lead to closure. Whatever the case, weddings often double as reunions. Ready yourself ("Mine to Make").

- For those working a wedding: Work and play can mix when the conditions are just right ("Set Alight").

Since I've already made clichés the theme of this introduction, tell me if you've heard this one: The difference between a comedy and a tragedy is whether the story ends with a wedding. Now, what happens when the wedding in a story is a foregone conclusion? Will there be laughter? Tears? Heartbreak? Violence? Romance? The following eight stories offer some interesting answers.

Charged Encounters

Petunias and Parenting at a Wedding

Carien Jordaan

UGH, WHAT A TERRIBLE WEDDING! WHO wants petunias at their wedding? And *One Less Problem* by Ariana Grande for the first dance...Is it just me, or does that send a mixed message? It is so typical of Chloe to try to be unique and then end up looking stupid.

I love my best friend, or I used to love Chloe but ever since she became friends with Byron... I should rephrase that; she was never simply friends with Byron. Those two were "complicated" from the moment they met. At least they have a proper label now: (uglily) married. And Byron and I were enemies at first sight. I saw right through his mommy issues, but Chloe loves to play mommy. We will see if she still loves the game when she falls pregnant.

I rush to the ladies' room to pull myself together. I stare at myself in the mirror and whisper, "You are the maid of honor at this reception! Act like you are enjoying yourself." I whip my head around as I hear a woman's laugh from one of the stalls. The woman leaves the stall and joins me in the mirror.

Oh no, my reflection betrays me by showcasing blood-red cheeks and a worried look in my dark brown eyes. Luckily, the reflection next to mine has adoring blue eyes with a grey shimmer that says, *Calm down*. Her low voice matches her eyes as she asks me to explain why I find this festive day rather unenjoyable. I explain the situation with the groom to her while she carefully reapplies her mascara. I notice that she uses an expensive brand of mascara and hastily grabs it when she offers the bottle to me. Now it is her turn to explain why she is hiding out in the bathroom.

"I do not know the people at this wedding. You see, I live in London. I am here on business, but I saw all the cars outside and decided to see what was happening inside. One could say I am 'crashing' the wedding," she chuckled, "Who is that middle-aged man seated next to the lady with the hideous hat?"

Byron's father is the complete opposite of Byron. He is kind, and he is always smiling. I find it sad that he raised Byron with as much love as he could after his wife disappeared along with all her belongings, and still, Byron turned out to be an awful person to be around. The woman next to him is his second wife, but they have only been married for a few months since Byron took up all his father's time and attention while he still lived with his father. I get the impression that Byron was a difficult child because it was his way of getting revenge. Chloe told me that Byron blamed his father for his mother's departure. It doesn't make sense because Byron doesn't even remember his mother – maybe she truly was problematic, and maybe his father is truly the saint that I view him as.

After the two of us gossip about the wedding guests and their funny fashion choices, she puts on some red lipstick, and I notice a colossal engagement ring on her finger! Just as I am about to ask her about the lover from London, she smacks her lips and then outers, "I'm parched; do you mind bringing me champagne?"

As I leave the comfort of the ladies', there are more questions dancing in my mind. Why didn't she want to leave the lavatory? Why didn't she have an English accent? Why did I not ask her what her name was?

But then another pair of adoring eyes distracts me. A handsome man makes his way to me. Very tall. Very well built. Very well dressed. He kind of reminds me of James Bond. We stare at each other for a good minute while I try to remember if I saw this face at the ceremony, but I believe I would have remembered those charismatic dimples. Another wedding crasher? Does this wedding just seem very approachable to wedding crashers? I guess the fact that the décor screams 'disaster wedding' attracts nosy people. Needless to say, I don't care. This man is the perfect candidate for a fling at a wedding reception.

He breaks the silence by telling me to dance with him. Well, technically, he asked, but the question sounded more like an order since he immediately grabbed my hand without waiting for an answer. I am grateful that he didn't wait for an answer because his voice melted my brain, so I would have just stood there like a puppet.

While we dance, I force myself to stop looking at him like a lost puppy looks at the first person who finds it. It's difficult, though, because I can feel people's eyes on us since he dances extremely well.

After a few songs, he pulls me to the table closest to the entrance. He offers to bring me a beverage, and then I remember … the champagne! After excusing myself, I run to the ladies' room, but the lady is not there anymore. I feel like a scholar who failed a test for the first time as I drag my feet into the reception venue and to the table where the good-looking man sat me down earlier. When I see that the table is empty, I feel like I just went to the next period and learned that I had failed another test.

The wedding was just starting to become less life-sucking. What a disappointment! And by now, most of the guests have had a few drinks and are trying to get into each other's pants. I can't help but pout while a slow song starts playing right on cue. Why didn't I take their contact numbers? The woman in the bathroom seemed like she could have been a good friend. I guess it wouldn't have worked anyway since she lives in London. I comfort myself further by convincing myself that the man probably wouldn't have been good in bed – he most likely knows that he is sexy, and the guys who know that girls swoon over them are the worst in bed. Too selfish.

Maybe I should leave early. The bride and groom have left already. And nobody here will miss me. I grab my sparkly purse and my pride as I stand up from the silly table. I hear my silly bridesmaids' heels click-clack faster and faster over the silly floor of this silly venue. When I get to the silly exit, I start rummaging through my purse. Where are my car keys?

Panic!

I sigh despondently because I register that one of my wedding-crasher friends was likely a thief. How could I be so dumb? Why would anybody be interested in me and my small life? Maybe I just felt lonely because today marks the day that I officially lose Chloe, and that made me desperate to find any person that looked at me longer than a second, to replace her. They exploited my vulnerability.

After a full 15 minutes of feeling sorry for myself, I try to cheer myself up by walking to the spot where I parked my beloved car. Maybe I merely lost my keys. Maybe there are still good people in the world who wouldn't take advantage of a defenseless bridesmaid. Not that I am defenseless; I am an independent woman. That is why I am walking all by myself in the dark to find a car that might not even be there.

As that exact thought crosses my mind, another thought runs past it: "Imbecile!"

I try to walk as fast as I can. Why did I park so far? I hear heavy footsteps behind me ... but it sounds like the person is taking very small steps – odd. I speed up. The person speeds up. Suddenly, the trees that looked picturesque in the daylight look like monsters. The pretty streetlights might be pretty, but they don't really shine that much light.

I might sound a little dramatic, but I am already picturing my funeral. I wonder who will arrange my funeral. My dear friend, Chloe, will be too busy with her honeymoon and her newborn since her man-child will exempt himself from any parental duties. Besides, looking at her flop wedding, I wouldn't want her to arrange my funeral. I sincerely hope it won't be an open casket funeral; those gross me out. I heard somewhere that one can have them plant a tree in your body when they bury it. That sounds more like me; I should definitely look into that if I make it out of this chaos. Mental note: Make up a funeral plan and leave it on your desktop!

Then the footsteps behind me stop. My curiosity may kill me one day ... or even today, but I must turn around to see what or who it was.

I can't believe it.

Chloe's uncle, Gideon, is intertwined with one of the waitresses against his car. Isn't she too young for him? And didn't his wife die only two weeks ago? I try to stay open-minded. True soul connections can't be defined by age. And people grieve in many different ways. I tell myself that I was judgmental at first. I was jealous because even Gideon is getting some kind of fun out of this wedding, and I'm (very single) walking to my car that might not even be there.

I found it! My car is right where I left it. And I found him, the James Bond man. He is next to my car! Is he trying to steal it? Should I walk up to him and tell him to leave my property at once? What if he tries to rob me or murder me? Maybe I should call the police. He hasn't noticed me yet. Thus, I believe I should turn around and run back to the reception hall. I will call the police when I get to safety.

"Hi, you dropped your car keys when you rushed to the toilets."

"Uhm, thank you," I reply awkwardly, not entirely sure what to say.

He laughs loudly before he asks me what my name is. After I tell him my name, he tells me that his name is Ruben. Mmm, fitting. After that, he asks me if I want to have a coffee with him at a restaurant nearby. The natural step would be for me to say yes, and then we jump into my car and go. But I am still suspicious ... didn't he come with a car? Doesn't he have a car? Is he unemployed?

After a moment of consideration, I decide to give him a chance, and we're off to one of my favorite restaurants – a humble joint; I hope he has an appreciation for small businesses like I do.

After we sit down in a dim-lighted booth, we start talking about everything from family issues to politics to hobbies to secrets to past relationships. We just can't keep our minds still. It's like our minds experience more chemistry than our bodies, not to say that our bodies do not feel chemistry. I mean, who wouldn't feel physical chemistry with that well-groomed stubble and gorgeous dark hair?

But now the waitress is approaching. She looks tired. But somehow, she still looks like she is trying to flirt with Ruben. She adjusts her ponytail while she tells us that the restaurant is closing, and then she puts the bill on the table. Before she can leave, Ruben asks for the card machine. She nods with a look of relief on her face, and then she turns around, swaying her hips as she walks to the cash register. Yes, she is undoubtedly trying to seduce him, but he seems blind to her efforts. His attention is focused on me. Some people would see this as a good quality, but I see it as a red flag! Because that means he won't tell women to leave him alone when they get too friendly; he will just act like he does not notice, and then they will try even harder.

It's like he can read my mind because that is when he puts his hand firmly on mine and gives it a little squeeze. I play coy by walking over to the waitress and paying my half of the bill in cash. He grins at me as I walk out to wait for him outside. Take that, annoying waitress!

He appears next to me.

"My place is not far from here. Want to drink some more coffee at my house? A midnight snack, perhaps?"

Time for some intrusive thoughts. House. He lives in a house, not an apartment. A sign of no financial struggle. What is his occupation? Does he rent the house, or does he own it? It shouldn't be important to me since I'm no gold digger ... but a successful man is attractive. Also, does this mean he expects to see what is underneath my dress? I don't hope so; I don't like going that far so early in the courtship. I am curious, though.

"Are you good at giving directions?" I ask as I get into the driver's seat.

His house is big but not a mansion – I like it. As soon as we get inside, he offers me a pair of sweatpants and a white T-shirt in case I would like to get more comfortable. I try to remember what color bra I'm wearing as I take the clothing from him, and he shows me where the restroom is.

Okay, I appreciate the fact that he is trying to be considerate of my comfort levels, but now I sort of feel like there is this expectation that I should leave this restroom looking like a Pinterest image, captioned, *Self-Care* or *Lazy Day* – a messy bun, no make-up make-up-look, and his shirt way too big for me. But my messy buns are always just that. Messy. Not aesthetic. And I don't have make-up remover. And my breasts will probably fill this shirt up, so no oversized look for me. Plus, my bra is black!

I try to tie my hair in a neat ponytail which is difficult without a brush. I wipe some of the concealer off my face with toilet paper. And I yank his clothes onto my body. I applaud myself for being such a quick thinker as I enter the living room.

Ruben hands me a cup of coffee as I sit down next to him. His couch is very comfortable. I wonder how many times he has had sex on it.

NO. No intrusive thoughts about his sex life!

I ask him about his job. He is a travel blogger. Interesting. That's probably why he said that his previous relationships didn't work out because they didn't see each other often enough. Another red flag. I am a receptionist at a dentist. I can't travel. Maybe I should stick to my original intentions – a fling. He puts his hand on my thigh, and I feel my heart racing. His touch is soft, but not the kind of soft that lacks grip, and I love the caring nature of his caress. It doesn't feel like a touch that is hungry for more skin like most men's physical contact feels.

The more we converse, the more enticing Ruben becomes. But at this point, I am exhausted from all the excitement that today brought. I can't help but yawn, and my eyes can't stay open for much longer.

I think Ruben has mastered the art of understanding the non-verbal communication women project because it is just then when he mentions that he is tired and would like to go to bed, but he ensures me that I am welcome to stay the night in the guest room.

We walk down the passage to the guest room. He shows me where the light switches are, and then he stands against me. His body against mine causes my whole body to get warm, and I lose my breath for a moment. He puts his face next to my ear and whispers goodnight, and then the heat all over my body turns into tingles. His big arms surround my waist. Every single muscle in my body relaxes.

"May I kiss you?" he asks underneath his breath.

I can't get a word out, so I simply nod. Then he gives me a very passionate kiss.

After a fantastic make-out session, he goes to his bedroom. I get into the guestroom bed. Wow, he sure is talented. And before my over-thinking can ruin the night for me, I fall asleep.

I wake up to the delicious smell of eggs on toast. I quickly use the guest room's ensuite bathroom to fix my hair. Luckily, there is mouth-wash in the cabinet, so I can get rid of my morning breath.

"Morniiiing!" I almost sing down the passage as I walk towards the kitchen.

"Good morning."

I freeze in the passage. My body goes ice cold as I hold my breath, and the muscles in my forehead tense so hard that my eyebrows feel like they are joining my hairline. That was a woman's voice. Not just any woman's voice. The same voice that laughed in the stall at the wedding reception's loo. The same voice that should have an English accent but doesn't.

Last night might have been like a dream, but it seems like today might just be a nightmare!

I don't know where to hide. I need a game plan. I will run back to the room and jump through the window. But just as I swing around, my eyes meet a man's chest. Ruben's chest. I can't even look up at his face ... I am too ashamed. Ruben's giggle calms me down, and I find the courage to look him in the eye. Even his eyes look like they are laughing at my confused facial expression.

"Come to the kitchen with me. I will explain," his voice soothes my ears that feel like they are on fire.

When we enter the kitchen, there she is, the wedding-crasher woman. She hands me a cup of coffee with a huge smirk on her face while I take a massive gulp. She introduces herself as Eirene, Ruben's fiancée. I should have known that he was too good to be true. Then she explains that they have an open relationship. Both of them travel a lot for work since she is the owner of a worldwide company. Sometimes they manage to align their work trips, and other times, they can't align their schedules which is why they decided to have an open relationship.

I have heard of people with open relationships before, but I have never been someone who's in an open relationship's conquest. This seems confusing because isn't the whole point of the open relationship to sleep with other people? Why would Ruben pursue me if I was not willing to sleep with him? There was real chemistry between us; it wasn't a one-night stand situation.

Finally, Eirene gives me some clarity. They are currently looking for someone else to join their relationship. When Eirene met me in the bathroom mirror, she thought that I would be a good partner. She texted Ruben, and that is when Ruben also wanted to meet me to spend some time with me. Even though I find the whole situation strange, Eirene certainly doesn't believe that flattery gets one nowhere. She keeps telling me how warm my aura is and that I seem dependable.

She picks up on my uncertain body language and changes her tactic by sounding a lot more serious and stating the facts. They need more stability in their relationship, and they think that inviting someone who has "homemaker energy," as she stated it, into their relationship will help. She proceeds to tell me what would be expected of me. They are looking for someone to be a stay-at-home partner in London. It sounds like they want someone to call home. The relationship would still be an open relationship. In other words, I could have sexual relations with other people, but it stops there; they don't have relationships with those people. For that reason, they only hook up with people once.

This is a lot of information to take in. Eirene knows that. She gives me their numbers and tells me to think about it.

I wish I could talk to Chloe about this. But now, I only have my four bedroom walls to discuss this scenario with. I am not getting any younger, and it isn't like there is a love affair on the horizon. I can see a relationship with Ruben. But I have always considered myself to be heterosexual. But it isn't like I find Eirene unattractive. Now that I think about it, I don't think these circumstances would be the best to raise children in since I will basically be on my own. The children's other parents will never be there. But it isn't like they are inviting me to be in a long-term relationship just yet. They made it clear that I can step out as soon as it doesn't work for me, just like one would in a two-person relationship. But I think that that means that I am disposable. The two of them are getting married soon, and where do I fit into that? Plus, I don't think I should try this if I know that this wouldn't work in the long run. I feel like I don't know enough to make my decision yet. I think I should do more research, but also many of the questions I have seem like they would differ from throuple to throuple because most of them are personal choices.

I pull my laptop closer but then...

Ding Dong! Ding Dong! Ding Dong!

I sprint to the front door. And to my surprise, it is Chloe.

"I don't know if I can marry Byron!"

I should have seen this coming. Only Chloe would be melodramatic enough to abandon her husband on the honeymoon and get cold feet when it is quite literally too late. Her make-up is smudged, and her hair is hidden away in a beanie. The poor thing probably realized that she is her husband's mother and feels like she needs a partner, not a child.

After 45 minutes of a flood of tears and mumbling that only she understands, Chloe becomes quiet. Suddenly a smile appears on her face. She has an idea. She is convinced that she isn't used to spending so much time with Byron and just needs a little break from the honeymoon. That sounds ridiculous since it has only been **one** night and who takes a break from their honeymoon? Your honeymoon is supposed to be a break! But I won't tell Chloe that. I know she won't listen. She'll just be offended for a few seconds and then tell me that she has always been unique.

I try to find some willpower to be Chloe's best friend for the day while I watch her take a towel from my cupboard and run to the bathroom. That is my sign to put a pin in my love life and start picking out an outfit for her because only certain items of my clothing fit Chloe, and they don't go well together. But I know her well enough to know that she won't go out in a mismatching outfit.

After getting ready and laying out some clothes for Chloe on my bed, she is still in the bathroom. My best guess would be that she doesn't feel comfortable enough around Byron to do anything other than urinate in the restroom when Byron is close. Another reason that they should have moved in together before the wedding, but Chloe thought it to be more romantic to yearn for each other from their own beds every night.

So, I type in "throuple" on my laptop.

And as Murphy would have it, Chloe walks in and sees my search. She shrieks and demands to know everything while she starts getting dressed. I explain the entire evening and morning to Chloe ... every detail. Her eyes are almost as wide as her mouth. I think this is the longest that Chloe has ever been quiet. I mean, she even talks in her sleep.

"That sounds like something from a movie—a sexy movie at that. Or no, something out of an erotic novel," she squeals while she claps her hands very quickly.

She gathers herself and slides my computer from my lap to hers. She asks me to make her coffee while she types vigorously. I have seen that squint too many times before. She is trying to stalk them on social media.

I use the couple of moments that I have to myself in the kitchen to recharge. Chloe is cool, but she can be tiring, especially when we spend 24 hours together. It usually feels like 24 days of non-stop chatter and shopping. My meditative state gets interrupted with a loud gasp from my bedroom. I breathe deeply to prepare myself for whatever is to come next.

She gives me a shocked glance as I enter the room. Then she stares at the computer screen.

"This is Byron's mom."

"Impossible. She's too young," I protest.

"She had him when she was 15."

I only realize now that Byron's father can be classified as a pedophile, but that is the least of my worries now. The only solution I can think of is to apologize profusely and promise to never contact them. How disgusting. I could have been Chloe's stepmother-in-law. Who tries to pick up a romantic partner from their son's wedding party? She must have known who I was and tried to get to Byron through me.

I snatch the piece of paper with their cell phone numbers from my nightstand, but then Chloe snatches it from my hands before I can tear it up. I look at her with a question mark on my face.

"We must find out what they want," she murmurs.

According to Chloe, I must tell them that I want to ask more questions at a coffee shop, and then we'll both be there to ask them what they want. I suggest calling the police but then remember that they have technically not done anything illegal. I guess Chloe's plan is the next best solution.

My stomach is deteriorating from all the stress while waiting for Ruben and Eirene. When they enter the café, they don't seem surprised at all – they must be good at casinos because those poker faces are immaculate. As they sit down, Chloe introduces herself and then follows with an explanation of who her husband is in an overly aggressive tone. Eirene and Ruben glimpse at each other, and then they look at me as if Chloe is not there.

As usual, Eirene does the talking. She explains that she lied about why she came to Cape Town. She wasn't actually in town on business. Her ex-husband, who she has been in contact with all along, informed her that her son was getting married. Her fiancé was already here for his travel blog, so she felt like fate wanted her to reconnect with her abandoned son. When she arrived at the reception, she couldn't bring herself to look at the men who she had caused so much pain in the eye. The meeting with me in the lavatory was 100% coincidental, and she unquestionably found an interest in me.

The next question rolls off my tongue without even thinking about it, "But why did you leave your own blood without ever trying to be in his life?"

Eirene starts tearing up, after which Chloe rolls her eyes. It is clear that Chloe is not convinced. Eirene's excuse is that she was too immature to have a child, especially with a man who was almost double her age. She felt overwhelmed because she fell deeply in love with this man who her friends and family did not approve of. When she fell pregnant, they kept urging her to abort and report him to the police. She didn't listen to her family for obvious reasons, so they cut her out of their lives. A few months after the birth of her sweet Byron, she grew lonely. All she wanted to do was send pictures of her baby boy to her friends or arrange for her baby to visit his grandparents. She struggled a lot as a new mother and lacked guidance. All these events lead to her doing the cowardly thing: running away. She did leave Byron's dad a note, and he understood where she came from. He made sure to still make her feel part of Byron's life by sending frequent photos and videos. The poor man waited for her to return, but the longer she stayed away, the more difficult it became to leave her new life behind. She apologizes throughout the story.

"Do you want to be in his life now, after such a long and painful time?" Chloe asks with no emotion in her voice.

Eirene bawls her eyes out while nodding, and Ruben tries to comfort her by holding her. Chloe slowly takes a pen out of her handbag and writes Byron's work number on a napkin. She doesn't say a word and nudges me to get up. We walk to my car in silence.

As soon as we get to my car, I interrogate Chloe. Why did she want to leave when we didn't get all the answers? Does Byron know she gave his number to his mom? Is she mad at Eirene? Or at Ruben?

But Chloe simply requests that I drop her off at the airport as she needs to break the news to Byron as soon as possible.

When I say goodbye to her at the airport, all she replies is, "How strange that it started out as a steamy film, and now it's turning into one of those books about family values that only old housewives read for their book clubs."

Rocketship Derivative

Penny Myles

Dear American Airlines:

I am writing to express my incredulity at your refusal to refund the cost of the ticket for my traveling companion, Sunny Lavalier.

We had only been seeing each other a short time, and I do not know her family, nor am I comfortable asking them for a death certificate, per your policy. She was 29 years old. Her death was tragic and unexpected.

While not a regular customer of American, I have flown many other airlines over the past two years and, without hesitation, received refunds or vouchers in the rare case of cancellations and emergencies.

Given the circumstances and in the interests of my future business, and general human decency, I hope you will

*find cause to grant an exemption to your policy and
refund the ticket.*

*Regards,
--Miles Gardner*

T HIS WAS, OF COURSE, A LIE.
He had been reading Hemingway while he sat at bars recently
and thought how both timely and untimely the old Abrahamic bastard
was— both of his time, behind and ahead of it—

when he told Ms. Barkley that he loved her in order to have sex.
This was as much about his manhood as it was her, the problematic,
typical extension of vaginas turned kingmakers.

Either not much has changed, or ever will, or there was something
tragically masculine and fragile and even honest, perhaps, about our
man-child protagonist Miles, who, using all of our most conditional
and cowardice qualifying phrases, let slip the specter of the L. word. *"I
think I might, but … I am not saying I— but."*

This was about a week before the wedding was scheduled, and she
used it as the excuse for her late about-face declination, uncertain and
scared off by those insidious words, that ineffable phrase unable to be
rescinded, overlooked, or tamed once let slip from the loose-tongued
hearts of naïve lips.

The truth was she got drunk on mushrooms and body rhythms
and White Claw seltzers at a music festival and fucked somebody else.
Likely, an old fling who had been helping her with the plumbing in her
new place, who she, in fact, likely had much more in common with, and
this was really the best for everybody.

He was always confusing orgasms with love anyway, as many tend
to do. Men, especially. Or at least, if not confusing, calling one name by
the other. And why shouldn't we, after all, rage against the disembodi-
ment of souls and quivering clits, soaked thighs, and pre-cum yearning

to be licked and send us spiraling to the multiverses' most delicate and sacred mysteries?

But back to our boy (Miles). Once, she had poured all over him the second time he went to visit—he had never been ridden so wet and long that her orgasm splashed his face with drops of herself—he swooned like a schoolboy first kissed, an over-eager student getting their first A+, Columbus's pettiest of naval officers laying first sight on a lush new land to be conquered and explored and cataloged, flags planted like that first time peeling panties down pelvic bones and beyond to the great, fantastic unknown between widening thighs.

Like the fatally flawed war hero, he felt more like a man for having made her cum so many times, that bed more drenched than his ego when she also awoke him with her mouth and moaned *so sexy* and licked every inch from him.

So yes, he did love her for that, as he should, although we all know she likely did not need him to achieve the high heights of ecstasy for which he needed her; but he loved her, nonetheless, for making him more of a psychic whole—and yes, physically fuller—version of himself. At least when they were together and naked. She had one of those deep, melismatic kinds of voices like a musician so that when she moaned would finish off anyone, as if the stars and stripes and atmosphere, more overheated than three industrial revolutions consecutively stacked against a newly birthed interstate and solar system and the mechanized car multiplied over a continent destined for high-rate emissions, all conspired to leave poor Miles defenseless— and she moaned frequently.

Both like and unlike Hemingway's shelled and hollow men, he too had told her he loved her out of a lie to keep and possess her as if he could own her pleasure, capture or remember or make it a part of him forever, but that in and of itself was the lie of manhood, and without irony, the lie of spoken love often turns into the real thing, and so it did. So, she made him pay for it, and now as far as American Airlines knew, she was, quite literally, dead.

No number of pages of curtly cut green hills or picturesque embraces or literary open-mouthed kisses could change that. Nor the most fervent redemption stories or ill-wrought romances slap away the slow sting of rejection, her shame at losing track of him and straying, the lie back of being repelled by disingenuous contrived heartthrobs, the simple rhythms of all this not changing the fact that he now flew south on a cylindrical metal bird ripping through invisible crosswinds and currents and clouds that rest assured, were very real and powerful, as most invisible things are.

He sat next to a pleasantly plain woman from Colorado and not her, and also not the beautiful brown-haired girl with leggings perfectly molded to her petite legs whom he had noticed in the concourse and who was now seated just out of reach on the aisle across from the old woman.

Far from fact, but fiction suiting just as well, the girl with the perfect soul juice pulsing pussy was dead, and Miles was going to the wedding alone.

Hemingway was writing symbolic landscapes from the nether beyond, while George W. painted wounded soldiers from some frozen little tributary two wrong turns off the road to the Greek underworld and hidden behind Pluto's sixteenth moon, and both still had holes in their heads.

When he landed, the flight attendant who looked Peruvian, perhaps, smiled at him, and he felt alright and changed his mind to the thought of seeing a rocket launch from the beach tomorrow before the wedding or the Saturday after.

That, too, was a lie. Her name was Olivia, and he had slipped her his number on a sliver of beverage napkin but knew she would not call.

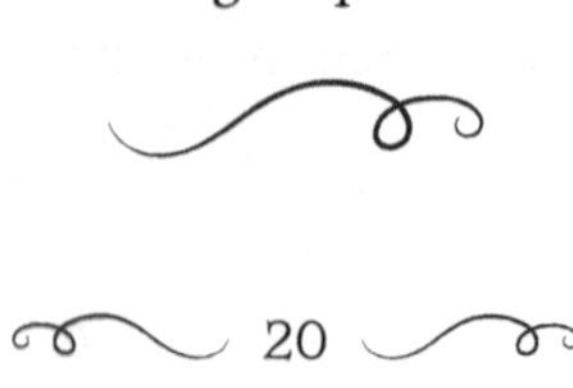

Upon landing on the so-called Space Coast, or at least south of it, Miles imagined a majestic descent through cotton ball clouds into a sea ocean of sky untethered by the nuisance of crag and mountain and granite he had grown so used to; instead, the sprawling green and post-WW2 gridded urban interstices rose like a great oasis to meet him through the clouds and still surrounded by the blue, and perhaps a fortuitous rocket launch propelling a shady unknown satellite or obfuscated scientific telescope against gravity and into space, the flowering smoke blooming like a gray technological mechanized flower reminding us of our place on this earthbound station.

There was also a man, not strange but unordinary, sitting caddie corner to the third left seat and triangulated between true North, the Prime Meridian, and the strange gray, slightly raggedy sport coat he soared in on that flight. The only things missing were the cigarette limply hanging from a creased, cynical mouth and some Salinger novel perched against a highball, neither of which are served anymore on planes— or at least not the fiction or booze in glasses.

It was a simple landing, and although the plane's brakes screeched, otherwise uneventful, but for the idiosyncrasy of the baggage exchange, which took too long and was manually delivered by scattering flight attendants whose training did not include the requisite bicep curls for this type of diminutive porter work.

By the time the second or seventh wave had washed over him, the only concerns remaining were the likelihood of shark volume per square oceanic yard and the reliable Florida sun on his skin. As like a loyal, enthusiastic dog, the foam lapped his face.

The day after the wedding, there was an intermission of idyl-island pastel green and Easter yellow beach houses interrupted by large, concrete block condominiums, par for the playa course on this, or really any, Florida coast after 1960 crossed.

Amidst the head-throbbing consequences of several rum & cokes, two beers, two glasses of champagne (one swallowed on the bus ride over), chardonnay sipped on the just-too-long shuttle ride back, a nightcap of two dirty martinis, and a tequila soda, and the mental rigor of then listing and cataloging the damage and degeneracy, he couldn't help but notice the gentle movement of the water in the toilet, the lack of calm even when undisturbed, that seemed to radiate the way a million invisible fragments come together to form a life, or parts of it, or tell a story.

Tropical Storm Agatha, trying at something eventful, undermined itself by its own expectation, or at least ours. In the end, the driftwood drifted, the tourists scuttled like superficial gulls in need of roosts, beaches evacuated to hotel rooms, and tikis were shuttered. Room service bills accumulated, and Uber trips were billed. The sand was now compact, as one would expect it to be. Washed-up sargassum remained, and slowly, the rare seagull returned to its foraging peck for what the storm ejaculated. The waves were still flummoxed and irritable and rolled over like white manes showing themselves to menace you when you looked at them.

He had decided to walk back after a most salacious brunch of shrimp & grits, and the two coquettish bartenders who were a strange simultaneity of too-young and too-old, and who amused him. There was a hotel called Cristal that made him smirk and think of Puff Daddy before he changed his name to whatever, and the walk was just long enough to require stretching, which was good.

There was also a dingier white and blue trimmed hotel as if a motel and the beach got into a squabble but, after great make-up sex, had something left to show for it, probably built in the 80s. The funny thing about reproduction and shells, I guess, is the same but always different, every time.

Hey, fellow beach walker— do you ever contemplate whether there's some kind of chip in your head or if you were a tragicomic invention of some superior sentient race or just an experiment in psychic surveillance, and no thoughts are interior thoughts, or private, or at least not yours?

Of course, you have, and that's called egotism, you espresso-juiced paranoiac. Once, it took somebody (not me, I'm not real) two years to read a Tom Robbins novel, and I still never dared attempt to hitchhike. The men seemed scary and singularly minded.

At this point, our nether-hero had walked so long down the beach, clear past his hotel, and the smallest frigate bird he had ever seen lit from a pile of seaweed and sea gargle so abruptly it scared both of their peripheries right out of their non-linear sockets and back into the Paleolithic age of mammalian vision. Back over and into the rough waves, he went gracefully. And back, the other, to his ungrateful tellurian stroll. And there were semicircular red, white, and blue banners left over from Memorial Day, two condos and one balcony over.

It was also a lie that he had passed the hotel. It was just a long walk, and the slow inertia of times' cruel limbo gateway had kicked in, as it often dies—does, each passing moment giving rise and end to the past and future, and so he still had a few minutes to go, pondering the rising of tides and the erosion of the public ideal, how one could be both Joe Biden and Aaron Rodgers vaccinated against the most terrible untimely of illnesses, as he had neglected to test as instructed before the wedding last night, and how the sea grape leaves were so circular and fractal and blew like their own lush sea up the beach.

The self-individualization and collective lie of humanimity, how in the end, we both fail and subsist to be a public, at odds both with ourselves and amongst ourselves in groups— like when an immune system turns on itself and attacks all the cells, both healthy and unhealthy.

And yet there he was again, the anonymous, eponymous master of the crossroads, a camp, shorted, blue hoodie frocked prophet almost hidden in the grape leaves, as if a hunched bird in mangroves. The invisible man perched atop a tall branch, slightly crouched, paring something from the bark, back turned, and it seemed this stranger must have known everything and nothing all at the same time.

When Miles approached, because, of course, in a story like this, he couldn't help himself, the crookedly awkward man did nothing. At first, nothing but elbows and a flicker of rondeau grape leaves circling the brownish body set firmly by the fluff of the surprisingly clean hoodie. But then he turned and spoke, it seemed, without saying a word.

The muffle seemed of the wind, or in spite of it, and went something like, "Whadya see walkin' by there." The man was clearly homeless, or crazy, or both, and Miles couldn't tell whether he was some derivation of redneck, migrant, or seer.

"Sorry to bother you, sir. What are you up to in there?"

"Seein' the leaves," he said curtly.

"What?"

"Seeing the leaves."

"You mean like reading the leaves, tea leaves?"

"Ain't no tea leaves round' here, boy. Just sea leaves and dunes. I'm pruning"

"Pruning for what?"

"Liftoff later. You ain't seen?"

"But that's ...."

"Never you mind. Rocket ships roar from unexpected"

And with that, Miles turned, saying no more to the crotchety man whose face was unclear even half-turned amidst the circular halos pretending to be leaves and who seemed to carry with him no determinate age. The pruning continued, seeming to make no progress. Although, by the posture and slant of the man whose limbs and actions arrowed out like vectors, it would seem he was trying to tunnel his way through the great sea bushes and make contact with a retainer wall, or eventually, some proof of still extant sand.

The ocean roared back alive as the soundproof balcony slider opened to the diminutive brownish green tufts of the over-pruned row of parking lot palm trees, still flicked horizontal by the windy remnants of Agatha, but the sun had re-emerged, and the rooftop A/C conductor units on the shorter adjacent hotel looked rusty and tenuously cobbled to their brackets, like the cringe of lost smirks. Miles brushed his teeth and descended to the familiar tiki bar. Robeson greeted him with that predictably warm and wide Haitian smile. His multiple ear piercings and formidable bling ornamented an otherwise short frame, uniformed by the requisite khaki and golf shirt formed by staff and, for that matter, most Floridians.

He would have one more swim in water less than 50 degrees Fahrenheit before returning to whatever he might return to, a New England future doling itself out in minutes and days, which would deny him that warm salt slurry and foam wash that baptized him like an invented sacrament on-repeat. It was feeding time, and maybe the sharks would eat him. Sometimes writing can be prophetic, but most of the time, it's not.

When he shook out his beach towel, the sand blew in the direction of the good-looking Jamaican couple, and he felt bad, but then realized they were fortunately uphill and untouched. As he passed them, the man smiled large because Miles had first glanced at the woman, and the man knew she was beautiful, and they both knew. He laid his towel on a chair at the tiki, rinsed his sandy brown feet, and ordered a beer. It was in this moment he realized he was a solitary person and preferred it. The hot Jamaican couple then sat at the bar, and it turned out the girl was from Georgia, and pregnant, and they were both very nice.

As he looked to the still conflicted horizon, he imagined a rocket ship slowly lifting across and up and above the waves, spewing a faraway eruption which would have been more violent and particulate up close. The rolling gentility of the clouds looked like huge breakers over the distant water and were deceptive. The real white caps were still there and omnipresent, rolling in and crashing like the sounds of so many stories and unwritten postcards patiently waiting for writing on their neat, rotational shelves in shops that sold more than cards or memories or knew anything of waves. Or the rogue ones that hit on less than deliberate occasions.

The beach was quiet and besides the quiet beat of Lil' Wayne pulsing from a nearby speaker, unassuming. The sand was still compacted from the last two days' anvil rain that had flattened it. The sargassum was still plentiful and dead and browning, and the waves still roared. A middle-aged man floundered to retrieve his dropped shirt while wrestling a towel, his sunglasses, and the lingering personal effects. That man was Miles, and after he quickly scuttled into place atop his flattened towel, the last corner of sun leaking through the Western sky and two condominiums, he was warm, and remembered he would need to buy a card and send the newly nuptial couple a gift, which he had awkwardly forgotten, but been honest about, and told them the truth the night before.

That night, he easily dispatched the first Heineken, suffering through the second when the surprising, almost startling, name danced across the screen of his muted phone that now gently shook atop the lacquered bar. He had an early flight back, which would inevitably see the plane's window, if he got one, ascending the diagonally tipped horizon as if hopelessly fleeing from the climbing star that burned its way into each day, which we call the sun. Sunny was calling him now, and he needed to free his undersized hand from the enthusiasm of paralysis which now engulfed it.

When he answered, it was her endearingly raspy voice, that deep, edgy, beautiful voice, uncharacteristically shaken.

"Hello..."

"Hey"

"Are you busy, it's loud"

"No, it's fine.

"I'm pregnant"

"What?"

"I know."

"How that's that..."

"I know. I don't know."

"What do you want to do?"

"I don't know."

"Is it still legal in NY?"

"Yes, but..."

"I don't know what to do."

"Okay, well I can..."

"I don't want to see you again. I'm seeing someone else. Please don't ask who."

"Can I call you when I'm back in a couple days?"

"Alright. Bye."

This was against all odds, logic, and luck, the literal biological, gravitational bodies and what and when we're capable, or just thrown together to see what sticks. They did not know what they would do, but at least she lived in New York, and at least she had had the consideration to call him, he thought and paid his tab.

Later, through balcony doors, the roiled and quiet hush of the sea put him to sleep, although the storm had fully and faithfully passed. There were still no satellite launches or aspiring lunar or Martian tacticians chomping at the sky for more space. Before closing his eyes, he carelessly packed his things in the fold-over hanging suitcase, then glanced across the room at the slick countertop, where two magnet cats stood golden and mane-less, the lioness placard table totems from the wedding the night before. Sunny's name had not been deleted from the place setting holder at the "find your table" station using corresponsive jungle figurines. These were chimpanzees and orangutangs, jaguars and cheetahs, and some elephants, and after he had thrown out her named placard, the twin lionesses, which he put in his coat pocket as a keepsake, non-descript as possible.

The conception had happened on Easter Vigil, to be exact. They had been tripping on mushrooms. And as they peaked, they watched the full moon hang over the lake in the upstate town where she lived, the glimmer refracting like exploding vibrations across the black expanse, their pupils full and black as eclipses and full of the looming Flower and Blood moon that would come in May.

In the end, the Atlantic continued to purr and roar, and blankets of white foam set well against the sea foam green and the murky grey sky.

The last day evolved into a prelude, and he missed his flight. Something about monkey bars. The clouds were cotton balls, and he felt the sheen thread count of the hotel sheets, realizing he missed every woman he had ever slept with, almost, and what a mess it would all again become.

Sunny, however, had two cats: Siamese Twins right out of the Disney childhood short of your childhood, if you were born in the proper eon. They were cute, actually— one would cuddle your feet when you attempted to leave, making it impossible.

In the end, he yet again read Hemingway at the bar, drank Peroni, which was fitting for the story, and watched the *Back to the Future* matinee, interrupted slightly by the Salinger story about tall girls playing tennis and refusing to eat ham sandwiches, and waste baskets full of sawdust and chickens and severed fingers.

Red flowers and scarlet begonias hung like small ornaments decorating the airport terminal drop-off, and the second plane was on time. The first one missed, of course, on account of the impregnable need to visit a reggae-themed pool join called Monkey Bar, get entirely too drunk, and helplessly hit on a beautiful lesbian couple at the toxic instigation of a large man named Robert.

This has become a sad story of multiple missed flights, and the tributary that feeds the Indian River is called Banana River, so the world still strives for organic unity. Also, they really weren't begonias, but he romanticized them as such. The second plane was on time.

The woman sitting across from him read some book about Floridian piratical bullion salvages or the Gold Coast or some muddling of it all, and rhetorically joked about not understanding the lead flight attendant on account of her accent. The second time she made the joke, I realized it was meant to be racist; the attendant's accent was never that thick.

There were no auspicious rockets cutting or floundering through the sky, only a baby blue whisp of occasional cumuli, the clouds clean and particulate and swept a bit gray and dirty in their middles. The intracoastal loomed through the plane's porthole window, and the clouds cast deep shadows down across the sea, themselves like white mountains or uncontainable waves spilling out and over the sky.

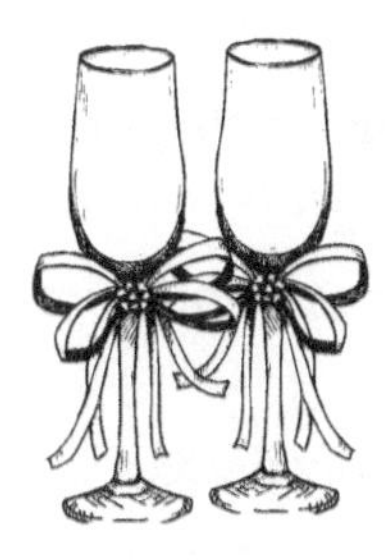

Stealing Cake

Kelly Fauth

I SMOOTH OUT THE BOTTOM OF MY DRESS FOR the millionth time. I know he's going to be here tonight – the man my best friend Gen can't stop talking about. Her best friend in undergrad. Well, besides her husband, Trevor, of course. Or should I say almost-husband. Because he won't technically be her husband for another – I glance at the clock on the wall – 45 minutes.

Gen has been going on and on about him for weeks. How he just moved back here, how funny he is, how loyal and reliable, how whenever she talks to him, it's always a long philosophical discussion about inequality and intersectionality. She must know that she's listing all the must-haves on my list of "qualities of the perfect partner."

"Hi, Annie."

Wrenched from my thoughts, I turn, my stomach doing jumping jacks. It settles quickly. It's just Joe.

"Hi, Joe."

"Fancy seeing you here."

"Ha. Ha." I roll my eyes at him. "Where's your beautiful girlfriend?"

"Oh, she's around here somewhere." He waves his arm in the air. "Did you find parking?"

It seems an innocuous question, but, in actuality, it starts us off on a ten-minute rant on finding parking in a downtown that's grown too quickly and changed nothing about its infrastructure.

"What are you two on about this time?" Joe's girlfriend, Frankie, has arrived.

"Oh, just talking about how perfect you are," Joe says in a sing-song voice. For his sake, I fight the urge to roll my eyes. Their lips meet, and I can't stop the spark of jealousy that hits me. Not because I want Joe or Frankie. I just want *that.*

"Uh oh, don't look now," Frankie whispers to me. "Chris." She nods her head behind me to the left.

I stiffen. "Is he coming over?"

"Um ..." She glances behind me. "Yeah, sorry."

"Is there time to ..."

"Hi, Annie."

Crap.

"Hi, Chris." I do not greet my ex-boyfriend with a smile, just a curt nod. Luckily, Joe saves me from further conversation by launching into a description of his latest bike ride downtown. A harrowing ride filled with killer buses and angry children.

Shooting a look at Frankie, I fade into the background. She nods at me, encouraging me to go. Looking around, I don't see anyone else I know. Maybe I'll head to the bathroom. That's always a good time killer. I head toward the doors I came in. I think I remember seeing a sign back there.

I'm looking up, searching for a sign, when my shoulder hits something soft. "Oh, I'm sorry," I say immediately, knowing I've hit someone.

The soft body turns, and my stomach flips.

"It's fine," he says.

I stare. It's him. It's definitely him. Gen's only showed me the picture of them together a hundred times.

"Um, hi. Are you Danny? You don't know me. I'm Gen's friend, Annie. I just - I'm not creepy or anything. She's just shown your picture a bunch of times, so…" I trail off, realizing that protesting my creepiness while rambling on to a stranger is not a good look.

He smiles. And it's beautiful.

"Hi, Annie," he says, sticking out his hand. "It's nice to meet you." I meet his hand with mine, marveling at how warm he is. He breaks contact first, a second longer than I think is proper. Or maybe that's just wishful thinking.

"So!" I clap my hands together, desperately searching my brain for something to say that doesn't make me sound like a stalker. Gen has told me so much about him, though, that all I can think of are things I know about him. He likes philosophy. He's good at riddles. He's funny and kind and—

"You come here often?" A lopsided grin sneaks onto his face.

I laugh. "Yes, I've been to Gen and Trevor's wedding many times. I'm planning on coming next weekend as well."

He laughs, and it might be the most melodious sound I've ever heard.

"Well, since you've been here so many times, what do you recommend as entertainment at this joint? And," he wiggles an eyebrow at me, "are the appetizers any good?"

"They're to die for, darling," I say, dragging out the darling like they do in old black and white movies. "And the dancing." I throw my hands up dramatically. "You've never seen anything like it."

"Well, in that case, I shall devote my mind to looking forward to that part of the evening."

"Danny!" A voice cuts across our conversation. He turns slightly.

"Hi, Carrie!" His voice is chipper, relieved. And Carrie is … beautiful. Damn. Gen didn't mention a girlfriend, but maybe she just doesn't know about her.

I wait anxiously. They embrace but don't kiss. So maybe not …

He turns to me, "Sorry, I—"

"No, it's okay. I should find the bathroom and then my seat anyway."

He nods, smiling just a little before turning away.

"How are you?" Carrie asks excitedly. I want to punch her.

I make a hasty escape, almost running to the bathroom. Why did Gen insist on keeping her bridesmaids family only? Then I could be hiding up there with her right now instead of in this bathroom by myself.

Pinching the bridge of my nose, I look into the mirror. My hair is down, medium-length and curly. My face is ... fine. Freckles, eyes that change from blue to green depending on what I'm wearing. And my father's nose. It's on the larger size. I'm not going to ever win any beauty contests, but I'm ... passable. I hope. Maybe he likes larger noses.

Whoosh.

I leap at the sound of the toilet. It's time to find a seat anyway.

I slide into a seat next to Joe. Fortunately for me, Chris is a row ahead and on the opposite side, seated with some friends he knows that I've only met once. Ugh. I can't believe he's here. I mean, to be fair, I knew he was coming. He was friends with Gen before I was. But our relationship was not a good one, and I've only just managed to get him to stop texting me. Keeping him away from me all night might be a chore. One I am not looking forward to.

I see Trevor slip into the front of the room, followed by his brother and cousin. The soft music in the background turns louder, switching into the classic "Here comes the bride." I guess this is it, then. We all stand and turn as the mothers of the bride and groom walk down the aisle, followed by the bride's two sisters and finally ... by Gen herself. She looks so happy. I don't know that I've ever seen her beam that much. As she moves down the aisle, I turn away from her, focusing my eyes on Trevor.

When I was in high school, I was watching one of those movies about always being a bridesmaid and never a bride. And for some reason, this one scene always stuck out to me. The main girl is watching yet another friend get married, and she turns to the person next to her and says, "This is my favorite part. Everyone always turns to watch the bride, but I always watch the groom. The look on their faces… That's what love looks like."

That's what I see now as I stare at Trevor. He looks enchanted, overwhelmed, and ecstatic all at once. They are perfect for each other, and my own heart swells at the thought of all of us coming together to support their love.

The ceremony is short, just over 15 minutes. I find myself wiping away a few tears during the vows and standing with everyone else as the new bride and groom dance down the aisle. Gen shoots me a wink as she passes me, wiggling her eyebrows suggestively. How can she know what I'm thinking? She can't possibly be suggesting what I think she is… Can she? It's the middle of her wedding! I put the thought away as guests leave their seats. The wait staff moves forward, grabbing chairs and moving small tables into place. This room really can do it all.

Wait, what? Did I just say that aloud?

I turn to the side. "This room really can do it all, can't it?" Danny repeats to his friend Carrie. He said it.

They are just a few feet away from me, and it's eerie hearing my own thoughts echo out of his mouth. I blink helplessly for a few seconds until he turns to me, shooting me his own wink. How is it so much cuter than Gen's? I have got to get a grip.

"Annie!" Frankie's voice calls out. "You're over here with us."

I move to my seat slowly, like I'm in jello or a very realistic dream. How did he literally say exactly what I was thinking?

"What's up, girl? You look like you've seen a ghost."

I force a laugh. "Luckily not. I'd be out of here faster than you could say … insert something clever here. I'm tired." I throw my elbows on the table as Joe laughs.

"Faster than you could say supercalifragilisticexpialidocious?"

"That'll work." I point my finger at Joe.

Another friend, Matt, joins us, along with his girlfriend, Parthi. There's only one seat left at the table. Oh god, I hope that doesn't mean… I scan the room anxiously. No, Chris is seated with his other friends on the other side of the room. God bless Genevieve.

"…chicken and green beans," Frankie is saying as I tune back into the conversation.

"I got the salmon," Parthi says. "What'd you get, Annie?" she asks, turning to me.

"I don't remember. But it doesn't matter. As long as there's cake."

"Oh, there definitely is." Matt leans across the table. "It's over there." He waves toward the corner of the room. "I don't know who made it, but I heard it's all chocolate with coffee icing. Mm." He puts his fingers to his lips and kisses them.

"See, now, no matter what happens, tonight will be perfect," I say, leaning back in my chair.

"Read 'no matter what happens' to mean Joe dances so hard, he breaks something."

"Hey!" Joe protests. "I'm a good dancer."

Frankie smiles at him as he makes a pouty face.

A movement to my right catches my eye. It's Danny, slipping out the side door to a cute patio filled with flowers. I wonder what he's doing. There's still at least 15 more minutes before Gen and the crew are done taking pictures.

I picture myself slipping out there with him. But that's too much, right? I don't want to ask my table because they will never let me hear the end of it. Still, now my feet won't stop tapping. I can't sit still. "I'm going to look at the cake," I blurt out abruptly, scooching my chair back.

"Don't steal any!" Joe yells to my retreating back.

I maneuver toward the back of the room where the cake lies atop a white lace tablecloth, pointedly not looking out at the patio. While I'm generally more concerned about the taste of cake than the appearance,

I can't deny this one is well-crafted. The piped-on flowers look almost real—so real my finger twitches, wanting to reach out and touch a petal.

"This isn't the most subtle heist ever attempted."

I jump as Danny's voice whispers near my ear. I stutter out a protest as I spin around. He laughs, taking one step back.

"If you're going to take off some icing, you gotta take it off the back."

I glare at him, both because he's stating the obvious and because he stepped back from me. Why did he do that? "I know that," I say, hands on my hips. "Do you think this is my first attempt at cake stealing?"

"I don't know." He shrugs. "Is it?"

"I'll have you know my dad raised me on icing swiping. It's just so much easier when it's birthday cake."

"Ah, 'cause then people are basically expecting it."

"Asking for it even."

"But not with wedding cake."

I heave a huge sigh. "It's eminently more difficult. I was just over here sizing up the situation."

"I interrupted the master at work then."

"Yes, you did." I glare at him again.

"I apologize." He places a hand over his heart, sweeping into a small bow. "How can I make it up to you?"

A thousand thoughts race through my head at once. I so badly want to answer that he should go on a date with me, or dance with me, or sneak off somewhere and—no. I shake my head. *Being creepy again. Don't do that.*

"How about you be my lookout when the moment comes?"

"Gladly." He smiles, still a step farther than he was in our earlier conversation.

"How's the weather out there?" I nod toward the patio.

He flushes a light red. "Oh, it's good. A bit hot."

"Yeah, men really shouldn't be required to wear pants as formalwear. Why can't shorts be fancy?"

"I agree," he says, looking relieved. "That's the double-edged sword of patriarchy, eh? Everyone gets trapped in roles."

"We just shouldn't have any boxes at all."

He smiles at me, a slow smile, almost as if he can't help himself. "I completely agree."

I tap my fingers against my thigh. I don't know what to say. We stand awkwardly for a moment. At least, I feel awkward. Maybe he doesn't. Maybe he stands silently with strangers all the time.

He clears his throat, and I think maybe not. He seems as uncomfortable as me. "So, how did you meet those two troublemakers?" He waves his hand toward Gen and Trevor, who are standing at a table full of Trevor's work friends, laughing and talking animatedly.

"Grad school. Well, I met Gen in grad school. We were lab partners. Trevor, I met later once we'd started hanging out more." I laugh, recalling one of my favorite Gen moments. "After a few weeks of school, she asked everyone in the program if they wanted to go on a 6 a.m. bike ride." Danny's eyes widen slightly. "I was the only one who said yes. And," I shrug, "the rest is history."

"You like bike riding then?" His eyes are bright.

"Yeah, it's fun to explore around town."

"Me too. I used to ride to all my classes in college. On the weekend, I would spend hours on my bike, just riding through town and exploring local trails."

"That's awesome," I say—because it is. I can't believe we both like biking. Gen didn't tell me about that. "And you met them in college, right?"

I already know this, but I'm still not ready to tell him that I know a lot about him while he probably knows nothing about me.

"Yeah, Gen was in one of my classes. She asked me to study with her one day, and the rest," he gestures to me, "is history."

Tap. Tap. Tap.

We look over to the middle of the room where Gen's Dad is standing with the microphone. "If everyone would take their seats, we're going to do a couple speeches and then the couple's first dance."

I look over at Danny, who gives me a half smile. "See you on the other side."

"I'll give you the signal when I need you."

He laughs, moving past me toward his seat. As he does, the faint smell of cigarettes wafts over me. Smoking. That's what he was doing out on the patio. That's why he wasn't standing near me. Normally, I am repulsed by smokers. I've been known to call them out in the middle of the street. I search my body for a reaction, but all I can feel is intrigue. I am so intrigued by him and not even the tiniest bit disgusted. Biting my lip, I make my way back to my seat. I'm really in trouble now.

When Gen and Trevor finish, Trevor yells out. "Alright, people, now everyone, get out here and dance!"

Matt and Parthi depart immediately for the dance floor. I can't go out there yet. They are the king and queen of dance and would put my silly moves to shame! I have to warm up to dancing. I know I'll go out there eventually. I'm just not quite ready yet. My friends know it, too, so they don't pressure me to come with them, just wave as they leave the table. I content myself with watching Joe and Frankie instead. They are hopping and flapping their arms like they're flying away. Laughing, I start to tap my feet. They are making me feel 100 times more confident right now.

"What are you doing over here by yourself? I thought you'd want to dance with your boyfriend." Danny's voice says from somewhere behind me.

"My who?" I laugh awkwardly, fighting the blush in my cheeks. I can't believe I recognize it already.

"That guy." He nods over at Chris, who is pumping his arms in the middle of a circle of people.

"Oh, him. Yeah, he's not my boyfriend. I mean, he was. Not anymore. I broke up with him."

"Ah. So just a jealous ex then."

My awkward laugh surfaces again. "I guess. I don't know."

"He's been hovering around you all night, so I just thought—" Danny cuts himself off with a shrug.

"Ugh. No. I just—" I glance around and then drop my voice. "I just got him to stop texting me the other week. He wouldn't leave me alone before that. But we have all the same friends, so I can't just avoid him all night. Then I'd be alone." I wince at how pathetic that sounds.

Danny's face lights up. "In that case, not only will I dance with you, but I can also be your new friend – hang out with me, avoid the ex. If you want to." He adds hastily at the end.

My stomach is doing burpees. Or star jumps. Something that makes it flip-flop around but in a way that makes me feel strong. *Does that make any sense?* I shake my head as I lead Danny out to the dance floor. His hand is warm in mine. I catch another faint hint of smoke as we walk, but I don't even care. Never in my life have I not cared about smoking. *Who am I? What's happening to me?*

I spin around when we get there, dropping his fingers. He immediately strikes a disco pose. "This is still how people are dancing, right? It was all the rage when I was a boy."

"And when was that, sir?" I ask, challenging his pose with one of my own, the 'Walk Like an Egyptian' arms.

"Oh, about 1962."

"You look awfully spry for one so old."

"I'm aging backwards."

"Ah," I say solemnly, "like Benjamin Button."

"Exactly." He winks at me before beginning the twist.

I laugh as I switch into 'the running man.'

"You're a fantastic dancer, you are!"

"I know! My mother was in the cabaret!" Our laughter bubbles up. My eyes are locked on his as the music shifts. A slow song. *Damn.*

He hesitates for a second, then holds out his hand. "Milady?" There is a question in his voice and in his eyes.

"Milord." I take it. Heat shoots through me, from his hand to my heart.

Tentatively, I take a step closer, raising my other arm to his shoulder. His hand goes to my waist, just above my hip bone. I might faint with glee.

"You know," I say quickly to cover my anxious nerves, "this is the perfect cover for our heist."

He gasps, looking around furtively. "You're right. We should keep spinning closer and closer to the table."

"We'll just look like enthused dancers."

"Instead of cake thieves." He finishes for me.

Wiggling his eyebrows, he steps toward the small table at the side of the room. I follow his lead, stepping with him before spinning him in a circle. He ducks down under my arm, laughing as he goes. Soon we're sidled up next to our target.

"Just one quick finger swipe around the back."

"Ah, but that's just the icing. For proper thievery, we need a whole slice."

I glance back toward the main part of the dance floor, where couples spin in each other's arms. Gen and Trevor are smiling at each other so hard I'm sure their cheeks must hurt. They have eyes only for each other.

"Excuse me." It's Carrie.

"Can I cut in?"

I look at Danny, stricken. He looks confused. "Um..." he stumbles and tightens his grip on my waist. The music slows and stops, changing quickly back to a high-speed banger.

"Sorry," Carrie looks at me. "I just thought I could use a dance to catch up with my old friend."

"Um, yeah, sure." I let go of Danny, stepping back. He looks at me, an indiscernible expression on his face.

"I'll find you later, Clyde." I smile.

He recovers quickly. "Bye, Bonnie."

"Are you having fun?" Gen appears at my side as I move back toward my seat. Her face is flushed, and a bead of sweat runs down her forehead.

"Not as much as you," I say with a laugh.

"What can I say? I was born dancing."

"I know." I smile at her. "This is great. Really. The food was good, and the dancing is fun."

"I know. I saw you with Danny." She bumps my hip with hers.

"He's nice."

"Just nice?"

I stick my tongue out at her. "Now is not the time," I whisper.

"Are you worried he'll hear us talking about him?" she whispers back.

"Yes!"

"Fine, I'll let you off the hook this time, but only because I'm getting married."

"Don't worry," I say. "Next time you get married, you can shout out my crush from the rooftops." Now it's her turn to stick her tongue.

"Okay, enough talk, Annie. Time to get serious." She grabs my hand, leading me back to the dance floor. We jump, wiggle, and move, surrounded by a mass of people all doing the same thing. Gen is in heaven, laughing and smiling at everyone she sees. Her enthusiasm is contagious, and soon I've forgotten about Carrie and Danny and am punching my fists in the air next to Joe and hip-checking Frankie. Chris is hovering behind me, but I put him out of my mind and concentrate on just moving my body.

Another slow song comes on. I duck behind Frankie, out of Chris's sightline, before heading back to my table for a drink. Sliding into my seat, I grab my water glass, smiling as I watch Frankie and Joe move together on the dance floor. They've only been together about a year, but they really seem perfect for each other. Maybe I'll be attending another wedding here soon.

"Casing the joint, are you?"

Danny appears, falling into the chair next to me. He came back to me. He sought me out!

I can't keep the smile off my face as I answer. "There's an old broad blocking the straightest route right now, but I figure if we cut into the corner where there's no security cameras first, we'll have a shot at it."

He leans back, drumming his fingers on the table. "We can't wait too much longer. The cake will be center stage soon."

My brain is still forging a reply when he changes the subject. "What're you drinking?"

I glance down at the forgotten glass in my hand. "Oh, rosé. What about you?"

"Water." He raises his glass to me. After a beat, he puts it back down. He doesn't look at me when he says, "I'm on a self-imposed ban from alcohol."

I already know about his alcoholism and his long stint in rehab. I also know that Gen said he's worked hard to rebuild his whole life, jobs and relationships included. But he doesn't know I know that.

"Well, most of it tastes terrible anyway, so I don't think you're missing much."

"You don't like it?"

"This rosé is about one of the only kinds I can stand, honestly."

He laughs. "I think you're the first person I've met who really doesn't like the taste. Really? Not even a sour beer? A pale ale? They can be good."

I shake my head. "Nope, basically just rosé and sangria. And even then, I'm mostly in it for the fruit."

"You're a strange one, Annie."

"Is that a dig or a compliment?"

"A compliment. Definitely." He smiles at me.

"Annie?" The voice I've been dreading all evening. "Can I speak to you for a minute?"

I want to say no. I really, really want to say no. But my mother always told me to be polite. Sighing, I get up. "Fine."

I shoot an apologetic look at Danny, who's giving me another unreadable stare. I follow Chris to a spot around the corner, toward the door where less people are congregated.

"What?" I can't hide the irritation in my voice.

"You look awfully cozy with that guy."

"So? What's it to you?"

"I just thought I'd warn you."

"Warn me of what?"

"He's a drug addict." His face looks so smug. I want to hit him.

"He's a former drug addict," I say, putting all the emphasis on the former. "He's better now."

Chris rolls his eyes. "So he says."

"I have no reason to disbelieve him."

"You have no reason to believe him."

"Actually," I say, my temper snapping, "I have no reason to believe you. You are the one with the ulterior motive here. I'm having a nice evening. Would you just leave me alone and try to do the same?"

He looks wounded, a look he perfected over the course of our relationship. "I'm just looking out for you, Annie poo."

My face curls up. "Don't call me that." I always hated that nickname.

"Let me help you."

"Okay, you can help me by leaving me alone."

"But Annie—" he reaches his hands out, but I'm already gone.

Stomping back to the table, I breathe easier when I see that Danny is still there. He waited for me.

"You waited for me." I didn't mean to say that out loud. This time I can't stop the blush that turns my entire face red.

He smiles. "Wanted to make sure you were alright. You didn't really seem like you wanted to go off with him."

I wince. "Am I that easy to read?"

"Only in that one instance." His grin is mischievous but tucked behind it is a seriousness.

"I'm okay. I told him to leave me alone."

"Good for you." He raises his glass to me again. "You're allowed to say no, you know. It might feel impolite but what's impolite is him forcing you into a corner."

He is a mind reader. Suspicion confirmed.

"I was always told it was mean to say no. I think that's why I stayed with him so long." And I don't just mean in our brief conversation just now.

Danny shakes his head. "Is it crueler to say no or to say yes but not mean it? To pretend you like someone? Don't they deserve someone who actually likes them?"

I turn my head, considering. "I think you're right. From now on, I'm going to make an effort to say no."

"Well, that's going to make my next question a bit awkward." He dips his head before speaking. "Do you want to stand next to me while they cut the cake?"

I laugh, "Yes."

While I was gone, they moved the cake table to the center of the dance floor and stationed Gen and Trevor strategically around it. Guests form a circle around them, all vying for the best view.

Danny and I walk up behind Gen and Trevor. We can't see their faces, but it doesn't matter. I know they're both smiling like mad.

"Last chance," Danny whispers in my ear. His breath tickles my hair, and I fight back a shiver.

"I think they've outdone us this time, Bonnie."

"They were on to us from the start, Clyde."

We watch as the happy couple feeds each other cake and poses for pictures. We cheer with the others when Gen wipes a dab of icing on Trevor's nose and then licks it off. As everyone heads back to their seats, Danny invites me to sit at his table. I slide into the chair next to him just as a waiter puts two slices in front of us.

"Would you look at that? They bring the goods right to us."

"Blend in with the crowd, pretend to be regular guests, and they just hand the cake to us. It's all about the long con, Daniel."

He laughs, taking a huge forkful of cake and shoving it into his mouth. "Well worth it, Annie, well worth it."

"Mission accomplished." Although now that it has been, I feel strangely sad. The cake means the night is coming to an end. I'll go back to my regular life, and Danny will go back to his. What if I never see him again?

"You know," Danny leans toward me, a conspiratorial twinkle in his eye. "I heard that couples get married in that park downtown all the time. Think we could put together a real heist now that we've had a little practice?"

My heart leaps inside my chest. He wants to see me again.

"Every good pair of thieves needs some easy gigs to get their skills up to par. I think we'll have to put together a lot of heists before we can really call ourselves good."

"That's gonna take a lot of weddings."

"Yes, it is."

"Good thing we found each other then, Clyde. It can only get better from here."

Oh, I hope so. God, I hope so.

I smile at him and decide to go out on a limb. "You know. We don't just have to practice stealing cake. We could also practice stealing food."

He pauses with his fork halfway to his mouth. "Whose food?"

"Gen and Trevor's or," I shrug, trying to make it casual, "a restaurant's."

Danny nods slowly, chewing contemplatively. "You know, I have heard that restaurants let you come in and steal their food as long as you show them this strange plastic rectangle at the end of your meal."

I laugh haughtily. "As if a plastic rectangle is worth anything."

"Exactly," he says, still nodding. "That sounds like the perfect heist to me."

I somehow manage to say the next sentence while holding my breath. "We should try it sometime." *Is that a blush on his cheeks?*

"Yes," he says. "Yes, we should."

Till Death Do Us Part

Jay Mendell

IT WAS A LOVELY DAY FOR A WEDDING. ELIJAH could admit that much. Light flooded in through the windows of the reception hall, a cheery spring morning awaiting them. Flowers, bright and cloying in their scent, were placed strategically around the room, both as decoration and as a quiet place for someone to duck away for a moment of peace, if so needed. A bounty of food was set upon the tables, ranging from the rich and decadent to a number of vegetarian and vegan options. There was even an ice statue of a swan as the centerpiece, its wings proudly held aloft as if in mid-flight.

All of these things would, of course, be infinitely improved if Elijah was allowed to make use of any of them, rather than being stuck standing by the wall with a serving tray, waiting for the guests to start flooding in.

Sometimes he wondered how he had ended up here, working minimum wage in service to people that had a net worth higher than his phone number, but then he sternly reminded himself that a job was a job, and he was the one who had decided to take it, so there was no use complaining. He knew exactly what his expertise was worth, and he would be happy to collect his earnings when this was all over.

Still, he thought he had the right to complain a *little* bit as the oak doors opened and the procession began to trickle in, starting with the photographer, quickly making his way through to get his equipment set up. Elijah resolved to keep an eye on his position—the last thing he needed was to get caught on camera here. Servers were supposed to appear only when needed and vanish otherwise, which was Elijah's specialty. After the photographer came, the wedding party—bridesmaids all dolled up with perfectly coiffed hair and the men wearing identical boring suits. Well, at least they fit the theme.

The bride and groom looked lovely, of course. Anything else would be criminal, considering how much they must have paid for all this. Rosy-cheeked, bright smiles. As they walked towards the dance floor, the priest waiting to give an announcement, they only had eyes for each other.

Elijah listened to the speech with only half an ear, eyes roaming over the rest of the crowd as they settled into their seats. Soon, he would be tasked with handing out drinks and taking any special orders, and it was good to get an idea of the layout now that almost everyone was inside, just in case he had to move quickly.

It was a lot of older businessmen and their wives—unsurprising, given the background of the lucky couple. No children, which he was silently grateful for. But other than that, there wasn't anything much of note—

Oh. Oh *no*.

What was *he* doing here?

Standing not far away, wearing a fancy, form-fitting suit, was Jonah Grimm. Someone who knew Elijah quite well and would be very surprised to see him acting as a server for a wedding party.

Elijah hissed under his breath, holding his serving tray up to shield his face as he moved back, diving further into the crowds. With any luck, he could be in and out of here without Jonah ever being the wiser—though exactly what Jonah was doing here was still in question.

There was no way he actually *knew* anyone at the wedding, and even if he did, why would he have been invited? Why would he have *accepted*? Elijah had never once seen Jonah in a professional enough capacity to be comfortable at a place like this. He was usually too busy dragging Jonah out of whatever dumpster he'd landed in this time.

The Best Man was speaking now, which meant there was just enough time for Elijah to sneak off to the kitchens and try to figure out—

"Hey, you!" a voice hissed, and Elijah stopped in his tracks, cursing his luck. It was the event organizer, a woman with thick glasses and long red nails—nails which were currently digging into Elijah's shoulder like talons.

"Yes, ma'am?" Elijah said, trying to hide a wince.

"What are you doing just standing off to the side? Get out there! Serve drinks, for god's sake!"

"Yes, ma'am," Elijah nodded stiffly and pulled himself away from her grasp, stumbling backwards towards the crowd.

Of course, in his haste to escape the demon that was middle management, he nearly tripped over the hem of a nearby tablecloth and stumbled right into someone, hitting their back with an *oomph*.

"Oh, please excuse—" Elijah turned to apologize to whatever businessman he'd just bumped into, only for the worst imaginable thing to happen.

"What are *you* doing here?" Jonah said, eyes wide. He nearly dropped his glass, and Elijah scowled as he held up a hand, making sure that Jonah's grip was secure before he let go.

"What am *I* doing here? What are *you* doing here?" he shot back, irritation lighting up his veins. The last thing he needed was for Jonah to ruin another one of his jobs. Bastard seemed to practically delight in the opportunity, and this time, Elijah was determined not to give it to him!

"I'm working," Jonah said, brow furrowing. He seemed to be just as startled by their meeting as Elijah was, at least, which meant that this wasn't something Jonah had planned to fuck with him.

In fact, if Jonah was here on a job, too, then that meant—

"Did you get hired by the father of the groom?" Elijah asked, feeling a growing suspicion. "Company president, bad toupee, smells like cheap cigars?"

"That would be the one." Jonah nodded, and the sour look on his face made it clear that he had also made the connection. "He hired you as well, I'm guessing?"

Elijah closed his eyes, working his jaw as he tried to suppress a bit of his frustration. "Yup. What are the odds, huh?"

The two shared a look and moved together to meld back into the crowd, crossing to the other side of the hall where they could hide among some of the greenery, giving them a bit more privacy—and, coincidentally, a clear view of the groom's table.

"So, either we're being set up, or this guy is an idiot," Jonah concluded, crossing his arms over his chest as he tapped his fingers against the champagne flute in his hand.

"I'm leaning more towards idiot," Elijah grunted.

What use would their mutual client have for trying to pull one over on them? It was far more likely that he simply thought he would have better odds of getting his way if he hired *two* assassins rather than sticking with just one.

"So ... what are we going to do about that?"

"Unless you plan on killing off the competition, I suppose we'll have to work ... *together*," Elijah spat out, even as his stomach wanted to rebel at the very idea.

"Yes, of course!" Jonah brightened, far too enthusiastic for a man that had once thrown Elijah off the side of a building because he was in pursuit of the same target. "That sounds absolutely lovely."

Elijah grunted, and there was a moment of awkward silence.

Now, they both understood where the other stood, but it was difficult to know where to go from there. They were hardly *friends*, after all, and there was a reason that assassins did their best to avoid crossing paths with each other—meeting up on the same job was incredibly uncommon, and for good reason; it almost always ended in a bloodbath.

Not, Elijah mused, that a bloodbath would be too ignoble an end for Jonah. Elijah bet that he could come up with something real nice—tasteful, even.

"You've got that look on your face again," Jonah said warily.

Elijah blinked. "And what look would that be?"

"The look that says you're already planning what to wear to my funeral," he said, and the suspicion in his narrowed eyes was entirely unpleasant, not to mention unreasonable. Elijah was a perfectly well-behaved member of society, side-job notwithstanding.

"It's cute that you think there'd be enough of you left for a funeral," Elijah muttered, and when Jonah shot him a wide-eyed, betrayed look, Elijah only stared him dead in the eye, raising a brow in question.

With a grimace, Jonah shook his head, visibly resettling himself. "Okay, alright, I get it. One of these days, you're going to kill me, and they'll never find the body."

"Or they'll never *stop* finding it," Elijah suggested. They'd done a bit like that once, during an earlier job in their career. It was pretty funny while it lasted, but he'd gotten bored of it quickly, so he'd just ended up dumping the rest of the body into the tiger pit at the local zoo and let them deal with that instead. Equally funny, if a bit less ominous than his original plan.

"You are a disturbing little man," Jonah said, entirely serious, and Elijah scoffed.

"One, I'm like, three inches shorter than you at most. Two, I sure hope you're not trying to take the moral high ground right now because I still remember our last dinner in Vegas."

Jonah grimaced instantly, proving that he, too, remembered that absolute disaster of a night. Elijah had lost three long-term clients because of that dinner. There would always be new ones to take their place, of course—that was the nature of the business—but it had still stung.

"Well, you don't need to go bringing *that* up," he grumbled, swirling his champagne. "Bad enough that Kris Emerson is still banned from every casino in the state. That was one of my more profitable identities, too."

"That's the nature of a gamble," Elijah pointed out, amused despite himself. Kris Emerson had been a fairly tolerable partner, so long as he didn't open his mouth and remind Elijah of who, exactly, was living behind the mask.

"Indeed," Jonah sighed, and then his eyes darted towards the groom's table, where there was movement happening. "Check your six."

Immediately, Elijah shifted his body slightly so that he had more cover and lifted his silver serving tray.

Checking the reflection, he caught sight of the groom standing from his table and holding out a hand to his beaming bride. Seems like it was almost time for the first dance—as soon as the couple finished giving their own speeches, they'd be out on the dance floor.

The father had remained sitting, and Elijah noted that *he* hadn't made a speech, which was perhaps unsurprising given Elijah and Jonah's reason for being here. The way the man was glowering at his son wasn't very inconspicuous, either.

Well, at least he didn't communicate with clients using his real identity, so when the old man inevitably got caught and started throwing out names to reduce his own sentence, there would be nothing to lead them back to Elijah.

"This is going to be an absolute disaster," Elijah spoke, lowering the serving tray and shifting into a more comfortable lounging position. It would be a while before either of them could make a move.

"No kidding," Jonah snorted. Then, he paused and turned towards Elijah, raising an inquisitive brow. "So, what was your plan, anyway?"

"I planned to poison his drink for the toast," Elijah shrugged, shifting the serving tray to hold it securely under one arm.

Jonah scoffed. "Oh, the one you're going to *serve* to him? And who will be suspect number one in a case like that, hm?"

Elijah's eyebrow twitched, and he had to work his jaw for a moment as he fought back his instinctual response, which would have involved a fair bit more blood than was typically acceptable at a wedding. "I told you the short version. My plan was a bit more complicated than just that."

"I'm sure." No one did condescension quite like Jonah did.

"Okay, genius," Elijah snapped. "What was *your* idea, then?"

Jonah lifted his drink, taking a delicate sip as if that would in any way hide the nasty little smirk that had sprouted on his face.

"Oh, an old classic," he purred. "The lovely couple steps out of the venue, so excited to drive off and begin their new life together, only to discover too late that there may be a slight issue with the brakes…"

He chuckled, swirling the champagne flute and looking every inch the rich, sadistic bastard he was pretending to be.

Elijah *tched* under his breath and kicked out at Jonah's ankle, causing him to yelp and hop backward, nearly falling into one of the obnoxious flower displays.

"What was that for?" he protested, and Elijah rolled his eyes.

"You were so happy to poke holes in my plan, but your plan has just as many issues!" he argued. "We were hired to take out the *groom*, not the bride, and anyone else that might have the misfortune to cross their path while they're trying to hit the brakes!"

Jonah waved a hand dismissively, placing his glass down on the nearest side table as he smoothly exited the range of any shrubbery. "In this business, some collateral damage is inevitable. A necessary expense, one might say. The fact that you haven't realized that yet only proves my point—"

"You went off on me for 'drawing too much attention,' and yet you think you're going to cause a five-car pileup on the nearest highway without anyone noticing?" Elijah shot back.

"Well, as a *professional*—"

"Um, excuse me?"

The two broke off their conversation, whipping their heads around to see who was interrupting—Elijah's hand darted instantly to the throwing knife hidden by his belt line, and he noted Jonah's fingers twitch in a similar manner.

The interruption was not, however, any mysteriously appearing cops or other lawfully minded nuisances. It was the wedding photographer, a young man with a thick beard and a sheepish grin.

"Sorry to bother you, but I need to get some cameras set up in this area. Would you mind moving?"

"Not at all, my good sir," Jonah said smoothly. Elijah cut a glance his way—that accent was laying it on a bit thick. "Please, don't mind us."

He got a hand around Elijah's upper arm, firmly steering him away.

Perhaps they *had* been talking a bit too cavalierly, but Jonah had started it!

"You're going to get us caught," Elijah grumbled, wrenching his arm away once they'd gotten to a safe distance.

"If this is the thing that gets us caught, we deserve it," was Jonah's conclusion, and Elijah shrugged with a half-grimace. As much as he hated to agree with Jonah, that was true enough.

Besides, the mix of people mingling and music blasting from speakers embedded in the walls meant someone would be hard-pressed to accidentally overhear them—and if someone *was* trying to interfere with their work, they would quickly find themselves with a few pointy objects shoved in uncomfortable places. Elijah would be happy to assist Jonah with that, at least.

"Look, we have to decide what to do," Jonah said. "Even if we both got hired, I doubt he's going to actually *pay* both of us."

"And it seems like you have better odds than I do," Elijah said darkly. "He got you in as a business partner, yeah? I didn't get an introduction. Had to throw together a fake resume just to get in the door. A *resume*, Jonah. Do you have any idea how long it's been since I've had to do shit like that?"

Jonah snorted and put his glass to the side, finally empty. Clearly, recent revelations had done nothing to dissuade him from drinking.

"And knowing your methods, you actually got the full scoop on his motives, right?" Jonah asked. "I didn't bother."

Jonah's 'no questions asked' policy gave him as much business as it did trouble, but the fact that the father had gone out of his way to ensure that he would know the location of *one* assassin while leaving the other up to chance...

"He's trying to cover all his bases," Elijah concluded. "Stupid way to go about it, though. If he was going to go through this much trouble, he should have just had his son arrested for money laundering. Would've been a hell of a lot easier than hiring us to kill the poor bastard."

"Is that what this is about?" Jonah said, sounding somewhat dismayed. "Based on all the subterfuge, I was hoping it would be something a bit more interesting. Like a secret bastard child interfering with the inheritance or a plot to take over the company from the inside."

"Nothing quite so grand, I'm afraid," Elijah said. "Which brings us back to the original issue. He's clearly trying to pull a fast one on us at some level. Are we going to let him get away with it? Or do we turn this around?"

"Hm..." Jonah stroked his chin considerably. It highlighted the sharp edge to his jawline, which Elijah instantly despised. The absolute *worst* thing a man like Jonah could be was handsome. "Well, I'm always up for a bit of fun, as you well know. What about one more job together, for old time's sake?"

Their 'old times' had often ended in blood and tears, which was not always intentional. But still...

Then, the music began to swell, a soft piano piece that let the singer's gentle croon echo across the hall, and Elijah perked up.

"First dance time!" Elijah hissed, poking Jonah in the side and maneuvering them closer to the dance floor. "We can take our shot after that."

"Not even time for a quick dance ourselves?" Jonah pouted. "It's almost like you're ashamed of me."

"I am not associated with you," Elijah said and promptly ignored any whining replies as he watched the proceedings with a keen eye.

The dance floor was clear, with only the bride and groom swaying back and forth underneath the glimmering chandelier overhead. When the crescendo in the song swelled, the groom twirled the bride with a deft hand, her laughter ringing as he let go, and she continued to spin a few steps away, her dress flaring out around her like a halo.

It was also at that moment that an ominous clinking sound filled the air.

Above the groom, the chandelier swayed violently, and with a great *snap,* it fell, crashing down on his head and crushing him instantly, leaving his body to twitch erratically in a pool of blood and broken glass.

"Huh," Elijah said. "Wasn't expecting that."

Predictably, all hell broke loose—the more surprising part was the bride pulling a handgun out of the front of her dress, immediately screaming for the culprit to reveal themselves. Not only did they *not* do that, but the high-pitched screaming echoing through the hall did nothing to hide the way a number of other guests immediately pulled out weapons of their own.

How had Elijah possibly missed this? Oh, right. He'd been distracted.

At least he could contend himself with the fact that their client looked just as confused about this whole scenario as Elijah felt and also like he had just pissed his pants. Unsurprising, considering that his son was currently a mushy pile of viscera and goo about three feet away from him.

"Oh, this has really all gone to hell now," Elijah complained, pulling out the small throwing knife he'd had tucked into the lining of his pressed pants.

But what else should he have expected? Everything always went to hell when Jonah was around. It was just a fact of life at this point.

"You never take me anywhere nice," Jonah said, with a hint of laughter in his voice, before he suddenly let out a strangled yelp, ducking down.

A swan head had just nearly given him a new haircut, the ice statue having promptly exploded into bits when someone lobbed a grenade into the display.

"Watch your head, idiot!" Elijah snapped. He shoved Jonah behind him, determined not to let the idiot crack his damn skull open and get blood all over his nice shoes.

"Hey, do you remember the first job we took together?" Jonah said suddenly, breathless and wide-eyed.

Elijah shot him a suspicious look and crouched behind an overturned table. "The one where you immediately tried to stab me in the back and make off with all the money? Yeah, I remember that."

Back in the day, it was considered easier on all parts to take cash rewards—Elijah knew better now. But even he had once been an innocent newbie, still so trusting in the better nature of humanity.

"And you tried to rip my throat out with your teeth," Jonah's voice sounded a touch dreamy. "I still have the scars."

Admittedly, Elijah had not been *that* innocent.

"What about it?" he growled, trying to keep one eye on his increasingly incoherent partner and the other on the standoff happening on the dance floor—the bride was in the better defensive position, considering that she had her back to the wall and couldn't be snuck up on by any enterprising idiots, but the photographer clearly had a layout of the place—his ʻcamera equipment was set up in some truly strategic locations. And—holy shit, was that the event organizer standing by the servants' door with a machete? Damn, no wonder he'd gotten such rancid vibes from her.

"God, it was beautiful, the way you laughed with my blood in your mouth. That's when I knew," Jonah said, proving that the delusions were growing more dire by the minute. "Elijah, I—"

"Do *not* say it," Elijah snapped. He refused to allow this—this *farce*! Especially not *now*, of all times, in the middle of what was possibly the worst op of his life!

"You're not the boss of me," Jonah retorted because he could not help but make himself a giant nuisance at any given opportunity. "So just *shut up* and let me—"

Thankfully for the sake of Elijah's blood pressure, he managed to cut this off before it could go any further by leaping out from behind cover and dragging Jonah behind one of the ornamental shrubberies, just in time to dodge a hail of bullets.

"This is really *not* the time to be having any kind of serious conversation, Jonah!" he yelled, peeking around the corner of the potted plant just to get an eyeful of blood spray as one of the guests went down. "Look, let's just get out of here, and then we can—"

Faster than he could react, Jonah grabbed him by the shoulder and pulled him back, a throwing knife skirting right past the tip of his nose. Elijah ended up sprawled out over Jonah's lap, looking up at him with wide eyes as they both breathed heavily.

Then, after all that, a smile broke out over Jonah's face, beautiful and wild—the kind of toothy expression that he never pulled out on a job like this. It was rare for Elijah to witness this event, and he realized very suddenly that he had missed it. Not missed it, perhaps, in the way of someone who had not seen it in a long time. But missed it in the way a drowning man missed the shore, uncertain of whether he would ever see it again.

"I would kill for you," Jonah said, and before Elijah could say anything biting to that piece of obvious news, he added, "For free."

Elijah couldn't help it—he blushed.

Behind them, someone yelled out a warning as a grenade went flying through the air, and the resulting explosion sent out a burst of wind that ruffled Li's perfectly tousled hair as if his pleading expression and concealed firearm weren't enough.

"Don't say something like that out of the blue," Elijah snapped, pressing a hand to his forehead as he tried to ignore the heat in his cheeks. "Once you kill for free, you're not an assassin anymore. You're just a murderer."

That was a hit to the reputation that no professional would be willing to allow—even most hitmen, who were far less picky about their client base than assassins, would try to refrain from wanton murder when possible.

"It would be worth it," Jonah swore, and when he reached out, Elijah didn't even stab him for having the audacity to tap his chin, pulling him closer. That was probably a warning sign; there'd be no turning back from here. "If it was you, it'd be worth it."

"You're just saying that," Elijah mumbled, but he couldn't deny the way that he was swaying closer, a sunflower growing in the direction of the light that sustained him.

"Then let me prove it," Jonah said and drew Elijah in, pausing with their faces so close they could nearly share a breath. "*Please*, Elijah."

Elijah let his eyes close for one moment more, cursing Jonah's unbearable sincerity and his own stupidity. Then he leaned in, pressing his mouth against the assassin who'd once tried to leave him for dead in the deserts of New Mexico.

And, well. Jonah still had the scars that marked him from that incident, so it was only fair.

Jonah was warm and soft against him, all loose-limbed and relaxed as he opened his mouth, shifting closer in a move that made Elijah's breath stutter. He tasted tart, like the terrible champagne he'd been drinking, and *god*, Elijah had never known anything better.

How long had he put this off, just because he'd been worried about professional integrity? As if Jonah had ever cared about that. He'd made it quite clear during their third time working together—when he'd gotten drunk off his ass and tried to convince Elijah that they should buy a lake house together. Elijah remembered peeling him off the bar top and throwing him into bed, dismissing the whole thing as the crazed ramblings of a drunk, but now he was thinking about it again.

They separated with a gasp when a nearby flashbang went off, causing a round of screams and both men to blink rapidly against the way that, even with their eyes closed, the world had suddenly lit up in front of them. Then, helplessly, they began to laugh, leaning heavily against each other as they shuffled to collapse behind another overturned table, ignoring the spattering of gunfire that ricocheted by their previous hiding place.

God, what an absolute *mess* this was.

But, Elijah considered, resting his chin against Li's chest as they sprawled out together, what else had he expected? This was par for the course for the two of them, and it was only bound to get worse from here if they continued to spend time together.

A lake house didn't sound too bad, actually.

"We should get married," Jonah said, breathless.

When Elijah wanted to say *what the hell are you talking about, that's stupid*, what actually came out of his mouth was, "With which identities?"

"These ones?" Jonah implored, looking up at him with big, pleading eyes. "Like, right now?"

Well, there *was* a priest in residence, and Elijah had seen him duck behind the pulpit at the front rather than pull out a gun, so there were pretty good odds that he wasn't a hired hitman, but—

"I don't think I want to marry this identity," Elijah said, scrunching his nose as he looked up and down Jonah's fancy suit, which, even when rumpled and pulled halfway open, still managed to make him look artfully sexy rather than the absolute mess he usually was.

"Not one of my better ones," Jonah agreed, though his shoulders drooped. "I just got it. Didn't think I would be using it for anything important."

"I don't want to marry a one-and-done," Elijah said. His current identity wasn't much better, considering he only used it when he was doing a job like this, and he tried to avoid customer service work whenever possible.

"Then marry me," Jonah persisted. "Just me."

Elijah exhaled shakily and propped himself up just enough to peek over the table. The bride had progressed to holding her new father-in-law (and their client, whoops) at gunpoint and was shouting at the best man to drop his phone—oh, someone's an undercover cop, huh? Tough luck, buddy—while the other bridesmaids lined up behind her. The maid of honor had looked a lot more dainty when she wasn't holding a giant club, but Elijah supposed that her dress was poofy enough to hide at least that much.

He ducked back down. "I think they're gonna be busy for a while. She is *definitely* a mob princess."

"Huh. Do you think the groom knew that?"

"Doubt it," Elijah grunted, and he kicked at the table leg to cover them a bit more when the screaming ratcheted up another level.

"So, this venue isn't available, then," Jonah said, visibly drooping in disappointment.

Elijah softened, leaning down to give Jonah a quick kiss before pulling back. "No, not right now. But we can find somewhere better. Somewhere less... messy."

"We should do it quickly," Jonah said. He sounded deadly serious, gripping Elijah's hand tightly. "

Elijah laughed and nodded. "Yeah, before I come to my senses."

And as the windows of the venue lit up with the multicolored strobe lights of oncoming police, Elijah and Jonah made their grand escape out the window of the men's restroom, laughing and clinging to each other all the way.

Jonah's suit was barely hanging on by a thread at this point, and Elijah was carrying a bottle of wine that may or may not be poisoned, but it certainly wasn't the worst end to a job they'd been on.

"We should do this more often," Jonah said giddily. His cheeks were flushed a fetching red, and Elijah just couldn't resist.

"Every day," Elijah promised. He pressed closer to Jonah, kissing him swift and deep as sirens wailed in the background. "After all, we're partners, aren't we?"

Resumed Encounters

COMPLIMENTARY BREAKFAST

Mimi Francis

ORA SAW HIM AS SOON AS SHE STEPPED into the resort's main building. It wasn't like she hadn't known he would be there, but she hoped she *wouldn't* see him until the rehearsal dinner or maybe, if she was lucky, not until the actual wedding. Unfortunately, luck was never on her side. She knew she would see him; it was inevitable. But she didn't expect it to be 2.5 seconds after she stepped out of the limo.

She ducked behind a giant potted plant and dragged in a deep breath. Her stomach flipped uneasily. No matter how much she tried to prepare herself, she wasn't ready to see him, let alone talk to him. Which was why she was hiding behind a potted plant in the plush lobby of the resort.

I need to get it together. He's just one man.

Except that one man was her walking nightmare. Walker Adams. The bane of her existence.

She and Walker had a tumultuous relationship. As the best friends of the soon-to-be-married couple, it was inevitable the two of them would run into each other. Frequently.

They were both single, and their best friends were dating. It was easy being around each other; they both liked to drink, dance, and party. Sam and Walker spent every minute possible together, much like her and Leila, so the four of them were together all the time.

At first, Sam and Leila encouraged her and Walker to get together; they thought it would be loads of fun if they were both a couple. For a while, it seemed like things might go in that direction. There was an immediate, mutual, and undeniable attraction. They hung out all the time, went out to dinner, drank, and danced. To no one's surprise, she and Walker became friends.

A year and a half after Sam and Leila started dating, they got engaged. Cora and Walker threw them an unbelievable engagement party—all the bells and whistles, friends, family, and co-workers. Tons of food and, of course, tons of alcohol.

The alcohol, the friendship, and the attraction led her and Walker straight to bed. They had an insane, intense, amazing weekend that rocked her world and ruined all other men for her. No one would ever compare to Walker Adams.

Cora quickly learned that Walker wasn't interested in anything more, like a relationship with her. He was only interested in sex. He enjoyed being her friend, liked hanging out with her, and loved having sex with her.

Except she wasn't interested in being Walker's fuck buddy. No matter how many times he asked. And he asked a lot. Every time she said no. It wasn't long before they both realized their friendship was over. Cora did her best to avoid him. That was six months ago.

Now, his best friend and hers were getting married. She and Walker were in the wedding party as the maid of honor and the best man. Cora thought she'd prepared herself for seeing him. Apparently, she was wrong.

Stop being a baby. Walk over there, say hello, get your room key, and walk away.

"Easy peasy," she muttered under her breath.

I'll avoid him as much as possible. If I have to, I'll hide in my room. He won't follow me there.

Cora grabbed the handle of her suitcase, straightened her shoulders, and stepped out from behind the giant potted plant. She crossed the lobby and eased to a stop behind Walker, who was gesturing angrily as he spoke to the man behind the counter.

"I think you made a mistake," he said. "I am *not* married. I am supposed to have a suite for myself. There shouldn't be anyone else in the room with me."

The young man shifted awkwardly, glanced at Cora, and held up one finger before he turned back to Walker. "I'm sorry, Mr. Adams." He pointed at the computer screen in front of him. "According to this, you are in a deluxe suite with your wife, Cora—"

"What?" Cora snapped. "What did you say?"

Walker swung around at the sound of her voice. He plastered a tense smile on his face, giving her a forced, pained look. "Cora, thank God. Maybe you can talk some sense into him."

"Excuse me a moment," the young man muttered. He scurried away and disappeared through a door behind the counter.

She waited beside Walker, neither of them speaking or even looking at each other. It was a tense few minutes until the young man returned, followed by a stern-looking older gentleman he introduced as the hotel manager, Mr. Pearson.

"What seems to be the problem?" Mr. Pearson asked, peering at them over the top of his glasses.

Cora cleared her throat and stepped up to the counter. She gave him her sweetest smile. "It seems we are in a suite together," she explained, gesturing to Walker. "Apparently under the mistaken assumption we're married. That is certainly *not* the case. We'd like separate rooms, please."

Mr. Pearson sighed heavily and tapped several keys on the keyboard. He squinted at the screen for what seemed like forever before he spoke.

"I'm afraid that is impossible. We do not have any extra rooms. We are completely booked."

"But—"

Pearson held up his hand, effectively cutting her off. "I'm sorry, ma'am, but there is truly nothing I can do. Either you share the suite, or I will have to cancel the reservation."

"Cancel the reservation?" Cora repeated.

"Yes. I can attempt to find you comparable accommodations elsewhere on the island, but I cannot make any promises. I can assure you, the suite we have available is quite large; it has a sitting room and an enormous bathroom. It's almost a small apartment. And we can certainly compensate both of you for our error."

Cora turned to Walker. "Leila will kill me if I'm not in the same hotel as her. Literally kill me."

"I guess we don't have much choice," Walker said. He turned to Pearson. "We'll share the suite. But if a room becomes available, please let us know right away."

"Of course, sir." Pearson turned to the young man. "Geoffrey, have extra blankets, pillows, and towels sent to room 1025. Get them two room keys and take their luggage to their room."

"Right away," Geoffrey replied. He snatched the phone off the counter and murmured into it while Pearson took their information.

Five minutes later, they had room keys and a voucher for a complimentary breakfast, the first step in "remedying our mistake" according to Pearson. The bellhop appeared, loaded their luggage onto a cart, and promised to deliver it safely to their room.

"I need a drink," Walker mumbled.

"Me too," Cora agreed. "Where's the bar?"

"May I recommend our poolside bar?" Pearson said. "It has a lovely view and wonderful drinks." He pointed across the lobby to a set of doors leading outside. "Go through those doors and turn left."

He cleared his throat and smiled. "I apologize for the inconvenience. Thank you for being so accommodating. I promise to make it up to you."

Despite Pearson's kind words, Cora couldn't bring herself to return the smile. They had turned her vow to avoid Walker as much as possible on its ear by forcing them to share a room. Now she would have to figure out how to live with him for three days.

I can make it through the wedding. I just have to get through the wedding.

Walker turned to look at her, a sweet smile on his stupidly adorable face. "I'm skipping the bar and going up to our room. Maybe I'll get room service, lie down before the rehearsal dinner. Why don't you come up with me?"

Cora raised an eyebrow. "Why would I do that?"

"I don't know. Maybe we can talk about why we aren't friends anymore. Clear the air." The smile turned into a smirk, and he winked at her. "Maybe we could kiss and make up?"

"Yeah, I'm sure you'd like that. Especially the kissing and making up part."

"I'm pretty sure you liked that part, too. If I remember that weekend correctly." He leaned close, his voice dropping to a whisper. "And trust me, I remember everything."

Cora ignored the goosebumps that rose on her skin and the tingle of desire shooting down her spine. She backed up and looked over her shoulder at the doors leading to the bar by the pool.

"I'm getting a drink," she said, spun on her heel, and bolted through the doors. Hopefully, Walker wouldn't follow her.

"Can I get another drink?"

The bartender raised an eyebrow, but he put another margarita in front of Cora a few seconds later. She wasn't drunk. Not even close.

Irritated and frustrated, but not drunk. Not yet, anyway. She suspected the only way she could sleep would be if she passed out.

"I don't need a hungover maid of honor." Leila dropped her purse on the bar and sat on the stool beside Cora. "Maybe you should slow down."

"I'm not drunk," Cora snapped. "I'm annoyed."

Leila glanced at her best friend out of the corner of her eye and laughed uneasily. "I heard. I'm sorry about the mix-up. Sam's in there right now, giving the poor manager hell. It won't get you your own room, but it might get us a refund."

"So, I'm stuck with Walker?"

"I'm afraid so." Leila signaled the bartender and pointed at Cora's drink when she got his attention. She waited until he set her drink in front of her before she spoke. "I know you're angry, Cora. I do. But I'm begging you, please don't make a big deal out of this. Sam is already on edge, I'm stressed beyond belief, and Walker is threatening to sleep on the beach."

Cora sighed and rolled her eyes. "Guilt? Really, Leila? You're going to use guilt on me?"

"I'll use whatever it takes to make sure everything goes according to plan. And that includes begging my best friend to suck it up and sleep with Sam's best man."

Cora snorted. "You're lucky I love you, Leila. Really lucky."

Leila exhaled loudly and rested her head on Cora's shoulder. "You're the best, sweetie. Literally, the best." When she looked up, her eyes sparkled with unshed tears.

Cora threw her arms around Leila and hugged her tight. "I'm sorry I freaked you out."

"I was afraid you would bolt or something. I know how you feel about Walker. I also know that seeing him at our wedding has been bugging the shit out of you. Now this? As soon as I found out, I came looking for you."

"I needed a drink." Cora sighed and pushed a hand through her hair.

"So did I." Leila held up her drink. She and Cora tapped their glasses together.

"To you and Sam," Cora said.

"Oh no," Leila giggled. "To you and Walker."

Cora groaned and downed her drink in three swallows. She slammed her glass down on the counter and closed her eyes. She could do this. She *had* to do this. For Leila.

For once, luck was on her side. Walker wasn't in the room when she went upstairs to take a shower. She dragged her suitcase into the bathroom, shut the door, and locked it. She took the fastest shower she'd ever taken, dried her short brown hair, got dressed, and put on a little makeup. Cora was in the room less than half an hour before she headed downstairs for the rehearsal.

She stood in the elevator, fidgeting with her watch and bouncing from foot to foot. She hadn't seen Walker since they checked in and had their brief confrontation in the lobby. She had to prepare herself for their inevitable reunion.

It came quicker than she expected. Walker grabbed her the second she stepped into the large banquet room. He tugged her into a corner behind another giant potted plant. She had a feeling her memories of this trip would include a lot of hiding behind potted plants.

"Hey," he said. "I've been looking for you."

"Did you try looking in our room by any chance?"

Walker rolled his eyes and gripped her upper arm. "Look, can we try to get along? For Sam and Leila's sake? I don't want anything to ruin their wedding."

Cora wrenched her arm away from him and bared her teeth. "Do you think I want to do anything to ruin their wedding? Leila is my best friend and the most important person in my life. I will do whatever I can to make sure this weekend is the best weekend of their lives. Even if it means putting up with your stupid ass."

"You're off to a shitty start," he snapped.

Cora pinched the bridge of her nose. "I'm sorry. You bring out the worst in me." She forced a smile onto her face. "I promise to be nice. Well, I promise to *try* to be nice."

Walker laughed. "I'm glad we're on the same page." He flashed her a sexy smile, his dark brown eyes twinkling. "Talk to you later, roomie."

Why the hell does he have to be so damn attractive?

Cora waited a few minutes to follow Walker. She joined him and the rest of the wedding party. Her best friend pounced on her as soon as she saw her. She threw her arms around Cora and hugged her tight.

"Are you okay?" she asked. Leila held her at arm's length and looked her up and down. She leaned close and dropped her voice to a whisper. "Hungover? Issues with Walker? Anything you need to talk about?"

Cora gave Leila her best smile. "I am fine," she lied. "No hangover. Things are fine with Walker, and no, I don't need to talk."

Leila nodded. "Good." She squeezed Cora's hands. "Let's get this rehearsal underway."

The next few hours were a whirlwind of activity—rehearsing for the ceremony, dinner, speeches, more speeches, and a lot of drinks. Cora was careful not to drink much; she stuck to water, only drinking when another toast required it. She kept one eye on Walker most of the night, but he seemed content to do his own thing, effectively avoiding her.

Not that it was intentional. At least, she didn't think it was. Walker was the life of the party. The guy everyone wanted to talk to and the guy everyone loved. He always had been. People constantly surrounded him. They sought him out and hung on his every word. It made Cora a little jealous.

She was relieved when Leila dragged her upstairs to her room and put her to work. She gave Cora a list with detailed instructions, determined—understandably—to make sure everything was perfect. Cora was more than happy to help.

It was one in the morning by the time she got back to her room. She eased open the door and stepped inside. The bathroom light was on, and she could see Walker on the couch. He appeared to be asleep. Cora uttered a silent prayer of thanks, ducked into the bathroom, and quickly changed into a pair of pajamas. She climbed into bed and was asleep seconds after her head hit the pillow.

Cora's phone vibrated at seven a.m., her signal to start the day. Despite her utter exhaustion, she crawled out of bed and made her way to the bathroom. It wasn't until she washed her face and brushed her teeth that she remembered she had a roommate. Cora cracked the door and peered into the other room.

Walker was still asleep. He was on his stomach, one arm and one leg hanging off the side of the couch. His pillow was on the floor, and his blanket was twisted around his ankles.

That can't be comfortable.

Guilt had her ducking back into the bathroom before he woke up and saw her well-rested face. She slept great in the enormous king-size bed. It never occurred to her that Walker was too big for the couch. She should have offered to sleep on it; she was about six inches shorter than Walker.

Cora slipped back into the bathroom, turned on the shower, and stepped under the hot water. She let her head fall back and sighed as the water cascaded over her.

She stood in the center of the bathroom wrapped in a large, fluffy towel, brushing her hair, when the door flung open, and Walker staggered in. He grunted in her direction, walked past her, and went around the corner. A few seconds later, she heard him going to the bathroom.

"Seriously, Walker?" she yelled.

"We slept together, Cora. No secrets. Besides, I had to piss. I must have had at least eight beers last night."

Cora stalked out of the bathroom. She kept the towel around herself as she dug through her suitcase for undergarments. Her dress was in Leila's room, so she had some shorts and a t-shirt to throw on. She glanced over her shoulder and listened carefully. The water ran in the sink, and it sounded like Walker was brushing his teeth. She'd have just enough time to get dressed before he came out.

Her towel fell to the ground, and she grabbed her panties. She had one leg raised and one hand on the edge of the bed to balance herself when she heard a low grunt from across the room.

"You should leave them off."

Cora froze, but only for a split second. She let the underwear fall to the floor and turned to face Walker. She stood tall, one hand on her hip, completely naked.

"You think I should go commando? Well, that would be pure torture for you." She sidled closer, a wicked grin on her face. "Do you really want to be standing a few feet away from me all day and all night, knowing the only thing between us is a thin, flimsy layer of fabric? That under that thin, flimsy layer of fabric, I am *completely* naked. Is that really what you want?"

Walker swallowed, his throat moving awkwardly and a slight blush on his cheeks. He opened his mouth, but all that came out was a breathy groan.

Cora moved closer. "I don't think you could handle it, Walker. Knowing that right under my dress was bare skin, skin you've touched, caressed, and kissed." She was inches away from him now, so close she could see a bead of sweat on his forehead. "Skin you will never have the pleasure to touch again."

Walker lunged, grabbed her by the upper arms, and pushed her backward until her knees hit the bed. They fell onto the soft mattress in a tangle of limbs, Walker on top of her. He grunted and shifted, his hips between her legs, pressing into her. He pulled her arms above her head and held her wrists in one hand and with the other hand, he held her chin, forcing her to look at him.

"What happened to us, sweetheart?" he whispered. "We were friends. You were my *best* friend. How did it all fall apart?"

"Sex, Walker. We had sex, and it ended our friendship—"

He cut her off, his mouth on hers, his tongue tracing her lips. The full weight of his body was on hers, and damn it, it felt good, felt right. She liked it. As Walker kissed her, her arm slipped around his waist and slid down his ass, tugging him closer. Her legs fell open, and the heavy weight of his hard shaft rubbed against her.

"It didn't have to end our friendship," he said. Walker cupped her breast and brushed his thumb across her nipple, bringing it to a hard peak. "We were good together. So, so good." He kissed her neck, delicate kisses that sent a scorching fire burning through her.

Cora closed her eyes. It could be good; she knew it could be good. There was no doubt in her mind that sex with Walker would be just as good as she remembered. But there were other things she remembered, too.

She put her hands on his chest and pushed him away. "I want to be more than your fuck buddy, Walker."

Walker sighed and released her. He climbed to his feet and adjusted himself. "Dammit, Cora. Is that what you think I want? A fuck buddy? Do you not know me at all?"

She propped herself up on her elbows. "I thought I did. I thought I knew everything about you. Then we spent one weekend together— one incredible weekend—and things kind of fell apart after that. Any time we were together after that, you thought we'd just fall right into bed. I had other ideas. We drifted apart, but we never talked about why."

"We didn't talk about why because you stopped returning my calls and avoided me."

He was right. She had avoided him. Cora pulled the sheet over her naked body and sat up. "Do you want to talk about it now?"

Walker snorted and looked at his watch. "I'm due downstairs in half an hour and I'm sure you have some maid of honor duties to attend to. We'll talk later." He went into the bathroom and shut the door. Cora heard the lock click into place.

She should have known he would avoid any kind of discussion. Serious discussions and Walker didn't mix.

She rose to her feet and put on her undergarments, shorts, and t-shirt. She stomped around the room, kicking stuff out of her way and throwing items out of her suitcase until she found her makeup bag. She grabbed it, as well as her purse, and headed for the door. On her way out, she spotted the voucher for the complimentary breakfast in the center of the table. She snatched it and tucked it in her handbag.

"I'm taking the complimentary breakfast, you ass!" Cora yelled at the closed bathroom door then she went out the hotel room door, slamming it closed behind her.

Two more days of this. Once this wedding weekend was over, she wouldn't have to see Walker again, at least not until Sam and Leila's one-year anniversary.

Cora fluffed Leila's train one last time, kissed her friend on the cheek, and stepped in front of her. She clutched her bouquet tightly and took Walker's arm.

Walker's breath was warm against her ear. "You look beautiful."

Warmth flooded her, as did the faintest tingle of desire. "Thank you," she whispered. "You look good, too."

Walker chuckled and straightened up as the music swelled. He put his hand over hers and started down the aisle, just like they'd practiced at the rehearsal dinner.

Cora silently chastised herself. Walker tells her she looks beautiful, and she basically says, "Oh, yeah, you, too."

He looked good. Unbelievably good. All the groomsmen wore charcoal gray suits with a red tie. Walker's fit him like a glove, emphasizing his lean stature and taut but subtle muscles. He had his dark blond hair freshly cut, and his face was clean-shaven. It looked like someone had the groomsmen pampered as much as the bridal party.

When they reached the altar, Walker kissed her cheek, lingering longer than necessary, then he patted her arm, released her, and moved to stand beside Sam. Cora smiled at him and turned her attention to the bride walking down the aisle.

Leila was gorgeous and seeing her sent a fresh wave of emotions rushing over Cora. She'd been crying off and on all morning; knowing Leila was happy meant the world to Cora. It even made sharing a room with Walker bearable.

Out of the corner of her eye, she caught Walker staring at her. Cora smiled at him, hoping he understood it was her way of apologizing. For one night, she would put any animosity she felt toward him away. She owed it to Sam and Leila. Walker returned the smile and added a wink.

The ceremony flew by. Photos were next, which meant a lot of standing around and being forced into awkward poses. She spent more time with Walker than she expected. She was relieved she decided to try to get along with him.

"All right, I think we're good," the photographer announced after an hour. "I'm going to head down to the pool and get set up."

Once the photographer was on his way inside, Cora helped Leila with her skirt. She lifted the train and buttoned it in place, making it easier for Leila to move around. Once she finished, Sam took Leila's hand and led her inside. The reception was on the other side of the resort, poolside. The hotel set tables and chairs beside two cabanas and the poolside bar. Cora joined the rest of the wedding party as they moved across the hotel. A hand on the small of her back brought her up short.

"Hi," Walker whispered.

Cora smiled. "Hey. How are you?"

Walker laughed. "I'm exhausted. You?"

"Same. But the night is young, and our duties are far from over." She shrugged. "Is your speech ready?"

Walker nodded. "How about yours?"

Cora laughed. "I wrote it the day after Sam proposed."

Walker chuckled. "You're always so on top of things. I love that about you."

Heat flooded her cheeks. She resisted the urge to fan herself. Instead, she buried her nose in her bouquet and giggled. Walker always had that effect on her.

He took her hand as they strolled through the hotel. She didn't pull away. She liked the feel of her hand in his, especially when it was so sweet, so casual. No ulterior motive. He held it until they walked into the reception.

"Do you want a drink?" he asked.

"Sure, how about a—"

"Rum and coke? Easy on the rum, right?"

Cora nodded and grinned. He remembered. There was more to Walker and maybe more to their friendship than she realized. She promised herself they would talk before the night was over.

Cora swiped at the tears streaming down her face. She didn't know why she was crying; it wasn't like she had gotten married.

She squeezed Leila tight until her best friend mumbled in Cora's ear that she was suffocating. Cora laughed and released her. Then she kissed Sam on the cheek before she stepped back and watched the happy couple climb into the decorated golf cart that would take them to the bride and groom's cottage at the back of the property.

Once they were out of sight, she turned to go back inside. Her heel caught in a crack in the sidewalk and her ankle twisted. The ground rushed toward her, but a pair of strong, sure hands grabbed her and steadied her, keeping her upright.

"Are you okay?" Walker asked.

Cora sighed. "Not really. I have had too much to drink. I'm emotional, and it's late. I'm tired, and I should probably go to bed."

Walker held her arm and led her inside. "Come on. I'll walk you to the room."

She yanked her arm free. "No. I want to go to the front desk. I want to get my own room. Maybe there's a vacancy."

"Don't be ridiculous," Walker muttered. "It's almost two in the morning. They won't have a free room, and besides, do you really want to pack up and move rooms in the middle of the night? Especially when you've been drinking?"

Cora shrugged, but she didn't answer.

Walker held out his hand. "Let's get you upstairs and get you to bed. I slept on the couch last night. I can do it again tonight."

She hesitated long enough to drag in a deep breath, then she took Walker's hand and let him guide her to the elevators.

Maybe I'm wrong. Maybe Walker is interested in me, and I've been the one running away.

It had been her choice to avoid him for the last six months. Six months that could have been filled with incredible sex, fun, and companionship. Just because their relationship started as one based on sex didn't mean it had to stay that way. Instead of turning her back on their friendship, she should have stuck around and worked on turning it into a relationship.

The elevator doors slid closed and instead of talking herself out of what she was about to do, Cora threw her arms around Walker and kissed him.

"Maybe you don't need to sleep on the couch tonight," she whispered.

What she didn't expect was for Walker to take a step back, grab her hands, and hold them at her sides. His brow furrowed, and he looked like he just drank sour milk.

"Look, sweetheart…"

Cora shook her head. She'd misread the situation. Walker was a gentleman, the consummate good guy. His offer to walk her to the room was because he was being nice.

"I'm sorry," she mumbled. "I'm emotional, slightly drunk, and I misread the vibe you gave off all night. Forget it happened."

She shifted from foot to foot and twisted the ribbons on her maid of honor gown around her fingers. She focused on the numbers flashing by on the elevator wall, resolutely not looking in Walker's direction. When the elevator stopped, and the doors opened, she flung herself through and took off down the hall, ignoring Walker calling after her.

Cora slid to a stop in front of the hotel room door and shoved the door card into the slot. The light flashed red. She did it again and then again, only to get the same response. She swore under her breath.

Walker's hand closed over hers, and his lips brushed the shell of her ear. "This isn't our room, sweetheart. Give me the keycard."

She handed it over and followed him down the hall to the door three down from the one she'd tried to open. She was an idiot.

Walker opened the door and gestured for her to go inside. Cora tossed her small clutch on the table and sank to the couch, her head in her hands.

"What was that?" he asked. "In the elevator?"

"I think I misread the situation. I'm sorry."

"What is with you this weekend? You're not acting like yourself."

"I'm fine," Cora snapped. "It's been a crazy week. I apologize for trying to kiss you. Isn't that enough?"

Walker sighed and loosened his tie. "I'm not upset you tried to kiss me. It took me by surprise. You've been avoiding me since we got here. Scratch that. You've been avoiding me for six months."

"With good reason," she muttered.

"What is that supposed to mean?"

Cora rose to her feet, teetering dangerously on her high heels thanks to the alcohol pulsing through her veins. She held onto the back of the couch, yanked them off, and tossed them aside. She crossed the room, grabbed a bottle of water off the bedside table, and gulped half of it. She turned back to Walker.

"I have been avoiding you intentionally. After we slept together, I got the impression you weren't interested in anything more than sex. I told you, I'm not interested in being your fuck buddy."

"Why do you keep saying that? Why on earth do you think that's all I want from you?"

Cora closed her eyes and sighed. "I don't want to talk about this right now, Walker. I'm tired, and I feel a hangover coming. I'm going to change my clothes and go to sleep. You can have the bed tonight. I'll sleep on the couch."

"Why don't we both sleep in the bed?" Walker said. "It's late, and we're both exhausted. It's a gigantic bed. I think we can sleep on opposite sides and behave ourselves, don't you?"

"I guess so," she muttered. She snatched her pajamas off the top of her suitcase and went into the bathroom. She slammed the door harder than intended. She changed, washed her face, and brushed her teeth. When she came out of the bathroom, Walker was in bed, lying on his back with his eyes closed, bare chest rising and falling. It looked like he was asleep.

Cora slid between the cool sheets and turned off the bedside lamp. She laid back and stared straight ahead, trying not to move or even breathe. The only thing she could think about was Walker inches away from her. The heat of his body seeped into her, and the smell of his cologne assaulted her. After a few minutes, he rolled to his side and faced her. She squeezed her eyes closed and tried to pretend she was asleep.

Walker chuckled. "I know you're awake. You're stiff as a board." He took her hand, his fingers intertwined with hers. "Can we talk?"

"What do you want to talk about?"

"Us."

Cora sighed. "There is no 'us,' Walker. There's you, and there's me. That's it."

"What if there could be? Us, I mean."

Her heart leaped. "Wh—what?"

"I'm wondering if there's a chance for us," he continued. "What if I want us to be together? I never got to tell you I wanted more. You assumed I didn't. You're the one who assumed I wanted a fuck buddy. You never asked if I wanted a girlfriend."

Cora took a second to replay the last six months in her head. She tried to remember when, or even if, Walker ever told her he wasn't interested in a relationship. She closed her eyes and sighed.

"You never... you never told me—"

"I never said I wasn't interested in a relationship. I don't know where you got that idea, but it's not true. In fact, I hoped we could have a relationship. I thought we were going in that direction, but you avoided me like I was the murderer in a horror story or something. I figured you weren't interested in a relationship with me."

Cora didn't know what to say. Her emotions twisted and turned, and her head spun. "Wow. Am I stupid or what?" she whispered.

Walker chuckled. "I don't think you're stupid." The bed shifted as he moved closer to her. His lips crashed into hers. He pushed the sheets away from her body, and he pulled her into his arms.

He growled low in the back of his throat. "Jesus, sweetheart. All this time, wasted." His tongue traced her lips and pushed into her mouth. He explored her with his mouth, tasting every inch of her. Their limbs tangled together, and their bodies were flush against each other.

When they broke apart, they were both gasping for air. Her body burned everywhere Walker touched, and a coil of want and need twisted in her gut. He put his hands on her hips and tugged her tight against him, his arousal evident against her upper thigh.

"How drunk are you?" Cora whispered.

"I'm not drunk at all. I had one beer and a glass of champagne. That was it." He brushed a kiss across her lips. "What about you? Are you drunk? Too drunk to know what you want?"

"I want you, Walker." She swallowed past the lump in her throat. "Do you want me?"

"You're all I've wanted since we first met," he whispered. He tangled his fingers in her hair, tipped her head back, and kissed her.

Cora relaxed into his arms with a contented sigh. The kiss deepened, her breath mingling with his, the taste of him filling her mouth. Her hands roamed over his torso, her nervousness and doubt replaced with her desire for Walker. All she wanted was what she'd always craved. Walker.

Walker seemed determined to take things slowly. He kissed her neck, his tongue sliding up and down her throat. He nipped at her collarbone and the soft skin behind her ear. His hands were all over— her waist, back, hips, the inside of her arm, the back of her legs, or caressing her face.

Cora caressed his chest and stomach, her fingers tracing his defined muscles. Her fingers slipped under the edge of his waistband, and she took him in her hand, stroking him slowly.

Walker moved over her. He took her breast in his mouth, and his tongue circled the nipple before he gently tugged on it with his teeth. Cora groaned and her back arched, pushing herself closer to his mouth. He wrapped his arm around her and held her as he suckled her breasts, paying equal attention to both. He kissed his way down her stomach and across her hips, then moved back to her breast. His lips were feathery touches and soft wisps of air on her skin, her body completely under his control.

A quiet moan left her when he slid his hand up her naked thigh and between her legs. His thumb pressed against her, circling her sensitive nub. The slight pressure drove her insane with need and desire.

She stroked Walker, giving him back some of the pleasure he gave to her. His hips moved as he thrust into her hand, low moans coming from the back of his throat as he continued to kiss her.

Walker eased two fingers into her and continued to rub her clit with his thumb. She was losing the ability to concentrate or think clearly because of the things Walker was doing. He was incredibly attentive, in tune with her body and what she wanted. Every touch inflamed her need, her skin on fire, her body screaming with want. She wanted him, and she wasn't sure she could wait much longer.

"Walker, please," she begged.

He pushed her legs open, nestled his hips between hers, and kissed her breathless.

She squirmed beneath him. "Condom?" she gasped.

"Shit, hold on." He pushed himself off the bed and stumbled around the dark room. His phone came on, and in the dim light, Cora saw him digging around his suitcase. The light went out, and he was back on the bed, kneeling between her legs.

Cora plucked the condom from his hand, tore it open, and eased it down Walker's shaft. She stroked him several times once it was in place. She wrapped her legs around his waist and guided him into her. He slid into her with a satisfied sigh, thrusting deep.

Cora moaned his name and rocked her hips up to meet him. She clutched his shoulders, her nails digging into the skin as she pulled him into her. She wanted to feel every inch of him.

Walker moved, thrusting hard and deep. He set a slow pace, taking his time to explore every inch of her. His hands were all over her body. His cock was buried deep inside of her, and his mouth was on hers, kissing her.

She was gone, flying, rocketing toward her orgasm, every thrust from Walker pushing her closer to the edge. She put her hands on his ass and pulled him closer, urging him to move. He slammed into her, pounding her into the mattress, her hips snapping up to meet his. Then she was gone, consumed by the sensations engulfing her as she fell to pieces. She came with a muffled cry of Walker's name and her face buried against his chest.

Walker caught her lips in a fierce kiss, a kiss that devoured her. His movements were erratic and intense, his cock pulsing as he came, a low moan rumbling through him. He continued kissing her even as he rolled off her and onto his back, pulling her with him. Cora snuggled close to him and rested her hand on his chest. His fingers drifted up and down her arm.

"Remind me to thank the hotel manager on our way out tomorrow," he mumbled.

Cora laughed. "Um, okay? What for?"

"For messing up our reservation," he said. "If he hadn't, I doubt we would have gotten our act together." He pressed a kiss to her forehead. "We wouldn't be together."

"Together? So, we're together?" Cora asked.

Walker chuckled. "I hope so. I've been waiting all weekend to get you where I want you."

"Back in your bed?"

"Only because I want you in my bed every night. What do you say?"

"I say yes." She giggled under her breath. "Maybe we should give the manager a complimentary breakfast like he gave us."

Walker snorted. "If I remember correctly, you took that breakfast, and I didn't get any."

"That's right, I did." She giggled. "I guess I owe you breakfast."

He tucked his hand beneath her chin, tipped her head back, and kissed her. A deep, probing kiss. "Get some sleep. I'll collect in the morning."

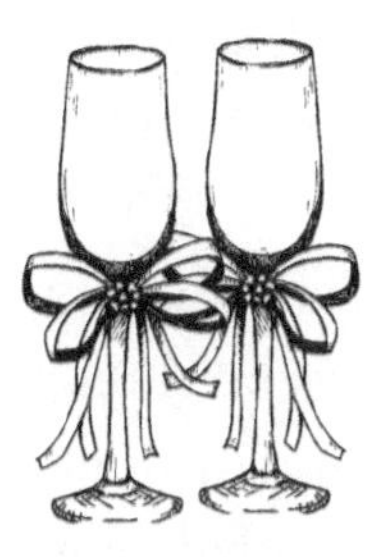

Could be Worse

Rebecca Grace

Chapter One – Jennifer

COULD THIS DAY GET ANY WORSE? Jennifer dug through her purse while searching for the stain stick she always kept. The wedding had been beautiful, but the reception had been one disaster after another. Her brother, Todd, abandoned her as soon as they entered the reception. His goal was to network with the groom's well-to-do cousins. Keeping his accident-prone sister out of trouble wasn't on his radar. Jennifer didn't know the bride or groom and accompanied her brother as his last-minute plus one. She tripped on a decorative floor runner, breaking the heel off her shoe as she entered the reception hall. The bride's creepy uncle, Bill, had pinched her backside as Jennifer limped to her assigned seat at the table closest to the wedding cake. She removed her shoes placing them on the floor next to her chair.

The bride's two widowed aunts, already seated at the table, glanced at her with pity. "Where's your boyfriend, dear? Why isn't he helping you to get settled," they asked. She replied that she had accompanied her brother to the wedding rather than a boyfriend. "You don't have a boyfriend? What a shame, dear. Every woman needs a good man." The aunts returned to gossiping about the bride, the groom, and the wedding guests.

Jennifer groaned when she realized that Bill was also seated at her table, along with his gorgeous daughter, Chantelle. Though they had gone to school together, Jennifer had never liked Chantelle. She was stunning, with her perfectly coiffed, blonde hair, perfectly manicured nails, elegant figure, and graceful walk. But Jennifer always felt like she couldn't measure up to Chantelle. Chantelle was independently wealthy but had made a name for herself through her health and fitness vlog. She seemed to feel it was her prerogative to delve into the fitness habits of those around her. Jennifer flashed Chantelle a welcoming smile anyway. At least she knew someone at her table. Chantelle nodded at Jennifer with a tight, half-smile, judgment of Jennifer's curvy figure in her eyes.

Bill ogled Jennifer from across the table. "You look great, Jen," he said to her well-endowed chest. "Make sure you save me a dance," he grinned, winking at her. Chantelle rolled her eyes at her father's drooling, clearly embarrassed by his behavior, and glared at Jennifer as if she encouraged Bill.

Jennifer held up her broken shoes. "No dancing for me tonight," she replied, grateful for a reason to turn him down. Bill continued to leer at her. She ignored his lascivious staring and Chantelle's disdain, turning to make small talk with the aunts.

Todd returned to his seat next to his sister just as the appetizers arrived. "You're looking well, Chantelle," he grinned. "How's the vlogging business?" Chantelle beamed back at him, his compliment chasing the disdain from her face. She proudly described the fun of promoting her fitness products and touting their success. Todd and Chantelle flirted as they ate. They discussed the healthiness of each appetizer available. When their entrees arrived, their conversation had moved on to comparing fitness regimens and local workout spots.

Jennifer's grilled chicken entree and vegetable sides arrived slathered in mushroom gravy. "I'm sorry to be a pain, but I can't eat this," Jennifer told the server as he set a plate before her. "I'm allergic to mushrooms."

"I'm so sorry," the server replied, "The bride's family was clear that no substitutions can be made. This is what was ordered for your companion's plus one." Jennifer glared at her brother. And pushed the plate aside. How could he have forgotten her one food allergy? Granted, she was a last-minute change as his expected date had changed her mind, but he should have at least offered to swap plates with her.

Todd was too engrossed in his conversation to notice his sister's discomfort. "Never mind, dear," one of the aunts said. "You won't attract a man while eating food like that anyway." Jennifer sighed as her stomach grumbled. Today had been the worst day ever. Now, it was going to be a very long night as well.

Chapter Two - Jennifer

This morning when Jennifer woke, her alarm blared a frantic, oversnoozed alert. She rushed to shower, only to shriek at the cold. Jennifer didn't have time to wait for the water to warm up. As she hurried to dress for work, she heard the sickening sound of shattering glass and splintering wood. Jennifer overheard the construction workers from the lot next to her apartment building cursing and knew there would be trouble. She peered through her bedroom door to a sight of utter devastation. The construction company must not have anchored their crane correctly. Its top had destroyed her living room wall and jutted well into her apartment. Jennifer's day continued to get worse from there.

Naturally, the accident caused her to be late for work. While she had never been late before, it was just the excuse her boss needed to send her packing. He had been looking for a reason to fire her since she'd turned down his romantic advances. With no home to return to and no job, she was forced to rely on her snarky older brother's goodwill until she could get back on her feet.

Jennifer's afternoon had been spent on the phone with the management of her now unlivable apartment building, attempting to retrieve her belongings from her apartment. After much hassle, she was allowed to come in only to retrieve irreplaceable items and her clothing. Jennifer had packed up her car and was making her way to her brother's residence when her car engine stalled and refused to restart. She had called a tow truck and then called Todd. He had complained but had helped her retrieve her belongings and had given her his spare room to stay in on the condition that she attend this wedding with him.

So, now she was obligated to sit at a wedding reception for people she barely knew with people she could barely tolerate. Her brother's date had ditched him last minute, and he felt it was important not to attend alone. "I'm looking for beta testers for my new summer slimline." Chantelle confided to Todd. "It's supposed to get you swimsuit-ready by June!"

"Jen should do it," Todd suggested. "She's between jobs at the moment. It might be the perfect project for her." Together, Todd and Chantelle scrutinized Jennifer. "Besides," Todd turned to Jennifer, "you should lose a little of that extra weight."

Jennifer frowned at her brother. "No thanks," she responded. "I like myself the way I am. And you seem to be planning to starve me over the next month anyway." She gestured to her plate. She waited for Todd to apologize, but he returned to flirting with Chantelle. Jennifer again engaged the aunts in small talk while Bill turned his ogling attention to her. Jennifer was polite but distant. She wished she could disappear.

Dinner dragged on; the conversation around the table continued similarly with Todd and Chantelle flirting, the aunts gossiping, and Bill leering. As the server cleared the plates and wine glasses away, he tripped over Jennifer's broken shoe, spilling red wine on her.

Though he apologized profusely, she waved him off and immediately began her search for her stain stick. She found it and treated the growing stain. She let the stain remover set and reapplied it while listening to the best man and maid of honor give touching speeches.

Then the dancing began. Usually, Jennifer loved to dance. Without functional shoes, she could only sit on the sidelines. The bride and her father showed off their fancy footwork with a cute routine before the bridal party joined in. Then the rest of the guests joined in the dancing. Todd stood and offered his hand to Chantelle. "Shall we show them how it's done?" Chantelle giggled and took his hand. Todd always thought he was smooth, but Jennifer winced, knowing how embarrassingly flamboyant his dance style was. Chantelle didn't seem to mind the extra dips and spins, though, and continued to cling to Todd despite the annoyed looks of the other dancers around them.

Bill approached Jennifer, but she used her broken high heel to wave him off once again. She sighed in relief when he chose to seek another partner elsewhere in the room. "Such a shame your shoes keep you from dancing," one of the aunts decreed. "You'd have better luck meeting a suitable young man on the dance floor." Jennifer bit her tongue gently to keep herself from rolling her eyes. The aunts meant well, even if Jennifer had no desire to meet a man.

"Well! If it isn't Calamity Jen!" came a deep, familiar voice from behind her. Jennifer looked around straight into a camera lens. "What sort of trouble have you gotten yourself into this time, Jennifer Jones?" Only one person had ever called her "Calamity Jen." It was just her luck that the wedding photographer would be the person she hated most in the world: Her brother's friend, Jeff Carson. Jeff had been her nemesis since middle school. He had constantly laughed at and made fun of her all through puberty. Jeff had been a handsome lad with a wicked sense of humor. His target had often been Jennifer and her clumsy scrapes. Any time she found herself in an embarrassing situation, he had been there. His ridicule had prevented more than one cute boy from asking her out. She had been grateful when he'd left for college and had hoped never to see him again. Yet here he was, pointing a camera at her regardless of her lack of shoes and stained dress.

"Living the dream, Jeff," she replied sarcastically, glaring at him. "Being the life of the party, as usual." Jennifer didn't think it was fair that, despite the activity of his job as the wedding photographer, he looked unrumpled and put together. "I've already worn out my shoes," she added. Jennifer turned back to watch the dancing, her feet tapping in time to the music. If her shoes hadn't broken, she could have avoided this conversation.

Jeff opened his camera bag. After a small amount of searching, he pulled out a tube of glue. "If you let it set for an hour, you should be able to dance again," he said. "Make sure you save me a dance after they cut the cake." Jennifer was amazed that he was doing something nice for her. She had expected derogatory comments like when they were in high school.

"I'll save the chicken dance just for you," Jennifer replied smugly, remembering his loud complaints about the dance in the past. "As long as I don't twist my ankle first. With the way this day is going, that seems likely. Thanks for the glue, Jeff." She handed the glue back to Jeff and set her shoe out of the way so that her repair could dry. Jeff fiddled with his tripod, trying to find the best angle to capture the cake cutting. Jennifer returned to watching the dancing. She looked for Todd and spotted him holding Chantelle more closely than she approved. Jennifer wondered if she would be homeless for the night due to her brother's romantic aspirations.

The dancing paused as the bride and groom moved to cut the cake. They'd chosen a military cake cutting to honor the groom's service. As the groom drew out his saber, he bumped the table, and the elegant 5 - tiered creation toppled directly toward Jennifer. She and other nearby guests rushed forward, attempting to prevent the cake from falling over. But it was no use. While the top 2 tiers were rescued by one of the groomsmen, the bottom tiers continued on their collision course with Jennifer. Being quite heavy, they bowled her over, coating her in red and white buttercream. The bride burst into tears. The groom consoled his new wife, reminding her that there was enough sheet cake to serve the guests. Jennifer had frozen in place, not sure what to do. Her vision was obscured by frosting, but she could hear the wedding planner arranging an alternate set-up for cutting a cake and the caterers rushing one of their employees to find piping supplies. Then someone handed her a towel and grabbed her hand, pulling her up off the floor and leading her back to the women's restroom.

"Seems like your typical wedding, Jen," her rescuer claimed, his voice amused. Just her luck, it was Jeff. He handed her a duffle bag as he hurried her into the restroom. "Sorry, I don't have a spare dress for you. My workout gear will have to do." Then he left her to clean herself up.

Jennifer wiped as much buttercream as she could off her face with the towel. She made her way to the bathroom sink, duffle bag in hand. Jennifer opened the bag and gagged as the workout scent filled the air. She pulled out a t-shirt and basketball shorts, sniffed them, and sighed with relief. The bag odor hadn't worked into the fabric yet, so Jeff must have washed his workout gear recently. Jennifer looked through the pockets of the smelly duffle bag and was grateful to discover a travel-sized shampoo bottle.

Jennifer turned on the sink, stripped out of her pale green dress, and removed the delicate necklace from around her neck. Then she went to work washing her hair in the sink. Once free of the buttercream, Jennifer finger-combed her wet hair and moved to the air dryer to dry it. She knew that without conditioner, her hair would be a curly, unmanageable mass, but at least it would be clean. Then she put on Jeff's t-shirt and shorts, rinsed out the buttercream from her dress, and cleaned off her necklace. While not very valuable, Jennifer was very attached to the four-leaf clover charm she'd had since she was a teenager.

She re-clasped the damp necklace around her neck and set to work attempting to tame her unruly hair.

Jennifer looked at herself in the mirror. While Jeff's clothes were baggy on her, she was grateful for the modesty they offered. She tightened the drawstring on the shorts, glad to know that they were in no danger of falling off. She had worried that his shirt would be too tight for her busty frame, but Jeff's shoulders must be expansive because the T-shirt seemed almost tailored to her. She wouldn't win any beauty contests in this outfit, but she was pleased that she was fully covered in clean clothes. For a moment, Jennifer considered drying her dress under the air dryers. The evening was getting late, and she knew that by the time she finished drying her dress, the reception would be over. There would be no point in wearing her fancy dress. Repacking Jeff's duffle, Jennifer went in search of a plastic bag to put her damp dress in. She was tired and hungry. It had been a very long day.

Chapter Three – Jeff

As a wedding photographer, Jeff had seen his share of crazy things. Alcohol and high emotions mix to create their own special brand of crazy. But he'd never before seen anything quite like the sight of the lovely, dejected woman sitting near the wedding cake. She frantically scrubbed at her pale green cocktail dress with one of those stain remover pens moms love so much. Her high heels sat beside her on the floor, one with its three-inch heel broken off. Jeff thought she looked familiar as he quickly snapped a photo of the guests at her table. He glanced at the man sitting next to her. Ah! Theodore Chadwick Jones III was better known to all his friends as Todd. At once, he knew the dejected beauty must be Jennifer, Todd's accident-prone little sister. Jeff and Todd had been thick as thieves growing up. Where one was, you could usually find the other. Todd had been a little pretentious and stuck up, but he and Jeff had always had a good time together. Jennifer, being younger, often wanted to tag along.

She'd been a little clumsy, and accidents seemed to follow her wherever she went. He remembered her as a cute, pudgy little kid who tripped over her own feet as she ran after the boys, insisting on spoiling Jeff and Todd's fun. They enjoyed teasing her, asking her what trouble she'd found each day. Jeff gave her the nickname "Calamity Jen." He never minded fishing her out of scrapes, though he enjoyed teasing her about the trouble she got into. Jeff always loved to find fun, and Jennifer always provided him with plenty of material for sport.

As a teenager, she blossomed into a beautiful young lady. She remained a little on the chubby side and continued to be accident-prone. He thought she was cute and sweet but off-limits as he was friends with her brother. He and Todd found endless amusement in teasing her about her various crushes and potential boyfriends. Jeff enjoyed making her blush since it was so easy. Then he and Todd left for separate colleges, and he hadn't thought twice about his friend's cute but bumbling sister. Now Jeff thought she was the most adorable woman he'd ever seen.

After capturing images of the best man and maid of honor speaking, he wandered through the reception, taking candid shots of the guests visiting and dancing. Jeff stopped now and then to chat briefly with guests he knew. At the appointed time, he made his way towards the wedding cake to set up his tripod to capture the bride and groom cutting it. Jeff noticed Jennifer sitting nearby with only two older ladies to keep her company. He wondered where Todd had disappeared to.

"Well! If it isn't Calamity Jen!" He raised his camera to capture her lovely face. "What sort of trouble have you gotten yourself into this time, Jennifer Jones?"

"Living the dream, Jeff," she replied sarcastically. "Being the life of the party, as usual. I've already worn out my shoes." She turned away from him, looking longingly at the dance floor.

Jeff opened his camera bag. After a small amount of searching, he pulled out a tube of glue. "If you let it set for an hour, you should be able to dance again," he said. "Make sure you save me a dance after they cut the cake."

"I'll save the chicken dance just for you," Jennifer replied, looking annoyed at the thought of dancing with him. She named his least favorite wedding dance. "As long as I don't twist my ankle first. With the way this day is going, that seems likely. Thanks for the glue, Jeff." She handed the glue back to Jeff. He returned it to a pocket of his camera bag. Jeff wondered why she disliked the idea of dancing with him so much. But he had a job to do, so Jeff focused on his tripod, trying to find the best angle to capture the cake cutting. He could see the groom pulling out his military saber in his peripheral vision.

Then all of a sudden, the cake toppled. Jeff grabbed his camera off the tripod and took picture after picture as the cake fell right onto Jennifer, knocking her over. The bride burst into tears, but Jeff worried more about his friend's sister than the hysterical bride. Jennifer looked dazed. But even covered in buttercream, she was adorable. He put his camera equipment into his bag and dashed out of the reception to grab his gym bag from his car. Jeff knew Jennifer would need a way to clean up and something to change into. He was glad he'd recently washed his gym clothes.

He made his way back to where Jennifer was still frozen. He handed Jennifer the towel from his gym bag, grabbed her hand, and pulled her toward the women's restroom. "Seems like your typical wedding, Jen. Sorry, I don't have a spare dress for you. My workout gear will have to do."

Leaving her to clean up, Jeff quickly returned to the reception. The bridal party had moved over to one of the sheet cakes that the caterer had prepared. Jeff grabbed his camera and took the cake-cutting shots he'd been requested to capture. There were only a handful of pictures left on the bride and groom's list. He still needed to capture pictures of the bouquet and garter belt tosses, but those were scheduled for later in the evening. Wondering why no one else had helped Jennifer, Jeff went in search of Todd.

Jeff found his friend, whose attention had been snared by a slender blond. While the lady of Todd's interest had dressed elegantly, she seemed plastic and aloof to Jeff.

Todd introduced them. "Jeff, this is Samantha's cousin, Chantelle. Chantelle, meet my good friend, Jeff Carson. Today, he's the wedding photographer."

Chantelle's chilly response left Jeff feeling patronized, as though she was above socializing with a mere photographer. However, he didn't worry about impressing her or correcting her perceptions of his care. Jeff was more concerned with alerting Todd to the predicament Jennifer was in.

Todd frowned at Jeff, seeming irritated that his sister's troubles interrupted his good time. "This is typical of Jen," Todd complained. "She's such a drama queen. I should have known better than to bring her along." Chantelle smirked and tugged at Todd, trying to pull him back to the dance. Todd sighed, "Do you think you can run her back to my place after she's changed?"

Jeff stared incredulously at his friend for a second or two. "I'm here to do a job, Todd," he declared. "I can't leave until I've finished what they are paying me to do."

Chantelle pouted and Todd huffed. "I suppose I can call her an Uber," Todd frowned. "The last time I put her in one of those, the driver turned up stoned."

Jeff glared, unhappy at his friend's dismissive attitude towards his sister. Jennifer deserved better treatment. "Look," he said to Todd, "once the bouquet and garter belt tosses are over, I'm free to go. I'll take her if you can't find her a ride by then."

Todd perked up immediately. "Thanks, pal! You've always been a good friend to me." Then he pulled Chantelle back to the dance floor.

Jeff shook his head. No wonder Jennifer seemed so down. He wondered why he hadn't noticed this sort of behavior from Todd in the past. Jeff snapped more casual photos of wedding guests as he meandered back toward the restroom where he'd left Jennifer. He needed to let her know that he was her ride home.

But Jennifer wasn't there. He knocked on the door, called out her name, and finally popped his head into the restroom, only to find it empty. He returned to the reception, keeping one eye on the time while looking for Jennifer. He still hadn't found her when the time approached for the bouquet toss. Jeff got his camera into position, his job almost done for the night. He'd find Jennifer when it was over.

Chapter Four - Jennifer

Jennifer crept around the edges of the reception hall, trying to be as unobtrusive as possible. She felt uncomfortable wearing gym clothes at such a formal event, even if the baggy gym shorts appeared to be a skirt on her. She stealthily made her way to her table, snagged her purse and her shoes, and edged around the room toward the kitchen. Wondering if her shoe repair had been successful, Jennifer slipped her shoes back on. While a little on the wobbly side, she felt the heel would hold up for the moment. Cautiously, she entered the kitchen, finding the kitchen staff in the process of cleaning up.

Jennifer managed to catch the attention of one of the dishwashers and asked for a plastic bag for her damp clothing. He found a kitchen manager who could provide Jennifer with what she needed. Grateful that something was going right for once this evening, Jennifer left the kitchen, keeping to the periphery of the reception. She needed to find Todd.

Knowing her brother would be upset at leaving early, Jennifer hesitantly scanned the room. The bride stood on the stage above the dance floor with a gathering of women below. Jennifer spotted Todd waiting on the other side of the group of women. With the focus on the bride, Jennifer decided to cross the room to talk to him. As she darted just behind the group of women, her head was struck by something. She reflexively grasped the object that hit her and gasped when she discovered she was holding the bride's bouquet.

She tried to pass it off to the nearest woman, but the crowd pushed her up to the stage despite her extremely casual attire. Face flaming, she stood on the stage, keeping her chin up. She refused to let her embarrassment create a scene. Then the groom delicately slipped the garter off his bride's leg. As the groom turned his back to the crowd of men who had replaced the women surrounding the stage, Jennifer scanned the room, looking for Todd. The crowd let out cheers and wolf whistles as the bride's Uncle Bill made his way up to the stage, garter in his fist.

"Looks like we'll be dancing together after all," he smirked. Jennifer glanced around, hoping to find an escape.

She spotted Jeff frowning at her from behind his camera. "Let me get a few pictures of you for the bridal album," he gruffly said, inserting himself between Bill and Jennifer. "I need one of you with the bride, Jen, and then Bill with the groom," he insisted.

Jennifer and the bride smiled for the camera, Jennifer hiding behind the bouquet. Then Bill and the groom hammed it up. Jennifer was grateful for a few moments of relief from Bill. But then Jeff ushered Jennifer into a pose next to Bill for the final set of pictures. "Let's keep these pictures clean," Jeff told Bill. Bill put his hand around Jennifer's waist and smiled at the camera. Just before Jeff pressed the shutter, Bill turned and kissed Jennifer on the cheek.

Jennifer's face flamed once again. She scowled at Bill, leaned in, and whispered in his ear, "If you EVER touch me again without my permission, I will kick you in the family jewels. Understand?" Bill glared back at Jennifer and took a step away from her.

After one last pose, Jeff ushered them down off the stage. On the top step, Jennifer's repaired heel broke loose from her shoe, twisting her ankle. Jennifer braced herself for the fall. But it never came. Firm hands steadied her at her waist and pulled her back toward a solid body. Jennifer looked around to thank the person who had come to her aid. Once again, Jeff had rescued her. Blushing, Jennifer thanked him as he helped her limp to a nearby chair.

Todd and Chantelle approached with faces like thunder. "How could you embarrass me like this, Jen?" Todd rebuked her. "Was it your intention to make me look bad?" Jennifer slumped, shaking her head.

"Your flirtation with my father has gone far enough," Chantelle hissed. "You look desperate, hitting on a man your dad's age."

"I've been dodging your perverted old man all evening," Jennifer exclaimed. "If anyone should be embarrassed, it's him." She shoved the bouquet at Chantelle and turned to her brother. "How does any of this reflect on you?" she asked. "No one even knows we're connected. You ditched me as soon as we got here." She turned her fury back on Chantelle. "You should take this dance with your disgusting father. I think I sprained my ankle. I just want to go home."

Todd glared at Jennifer and escorted Chantelle back to the dance floor. Jennifer sat back in her chair with a sigh, relieved that they had left. But she soon discovered she wasn't entirely alone. "When did your brother get to be such a jerk?" Jeff asked her as he knelt to check her injured ankle.

Jennifer looked at him in shock. "He's always been this way," she replied. "And you've never been much better. I'm surprised you're not already getting your digs in. I'm really not looking forward to the drive home with him."

"About that," Jeff interjected, "I'm your ride. Let me pack up my camera gear. Then, as soon as you're ready, we can go. Can you walk?" Jennifer removed her broken shoes again and cautiously stood up, testing her ankle. It more than twinged when she put weight on it, and she gasped in pain. "I think you better sit down again. I'll pack up my car and take you to the ER," Jeff insisted.

Jennifer felt astonished at his kind tone and behavior. She was puzzled over this change in her nemesis. She watched Chantelle dance with her father, pondering Jeff's sudden gallantry. Meanwhile, Todd glared at Jennifer from the edge of the dance floor. She knew she'd have an earful from him later this evening when he got home. She hoped Jeff wouldn't tease her too much when he returned.

CHAPTER FIVE - JEFF

Jeff stood near the stage, his camera ready as the familiar sound of Beyonce's "All the Single Ladies" pulsed through the air. The bride danced onto the stage to the cheers of her single friends gathered below. The DJ cut the music while Jeff snapped a series of pictures of the bride and her bouquet's flight through the air. Jeff smiled at the loud gasp from the woman who'd caught the bouquet, clearly surprised she'd been so lucky. The crowd pushed forward a woman in a t-shirt and gym shorts. Jen! The poor girl's face flushed beet red as she was urged onto the stage, clearly embarrassed at the spotlight.

Jeff admired how Jennifer kept her chin up, refusing to hide despite her embarrassment. The DJ spun up Hot Chocolate's "You Sexy Thing" as the groom helped his bride to a chair on the stage. Jeff snapped another series of shots of the groom carefully slipping the garter from his wife's leg, swinging it around his head, turning his back to the group below the stage, and tossing the garter backward. The crowd let out cheers and wolf whistles as the bride's Uncle Bill made his way up to the stage, garter in his fist.

Jeff frowned. Bill was a notorious lech. "Looks like we'll be dancing together, after all," Jeff heard him declare. Bill leered at Jennifer. Jeff shuddered under a sudden need to protect her from Bill's overtures.

"Let me get a few pictures of you for the bridal album," he gruffly said, inserting himself between Bill and Jennifer. "I need one of you with the bride, Jen, and then Bill with the groom," he insisted.

Jeff set up a pose for Jennifer and the bride, using the massive bouquet to disguise Jennifer's informal clothing. Though they smiled for the camera, Jeff could see neither was particularly happy.

Then the groom, having a comical bent, struck up a pose with Bill. Jeff took one picture with them both holding the garter, another with Bill "stealing" the garter from the groom, and a third with the groom removing the garter from Bill's leg. The groom's sense of humor kept the poses coming.

When the bride indicated they'd posed enough, Jeff called Jennifer back to pose next to Bill for the final set of pictures. If Bill was going to harass Jennifer, this would be his window of opportunity. "Let's keep these pictures clean," Jeff said to Bill, trying to prevent her any more embarrassment this evening. Bill put his hand around Jennifer's waist and smiled at the camera. Just before Jeff pressed the shutter, Bill turned and kissed Jennifer on the cheek.

Jennifer's face turned red with anger. Jeff watched as she leaned over and whispered something in Bill's ear. Bill took a step away from Jennifer and glared daggers at her. Jeff smiled. He was proud of her for standing up for herself. Jeff set a pose for them one last time and then ushered them off the stage for the bouquet and garter toss dance. He walked just behind Jennifer, protecting her from any more lecherous behavior by Bill. When she approached the top stair, she stumbled and began to fall. Jeff reached out and grabbed her waist, pulling her back into himself. She thanked him, blushing.

He helped her limp down the stairs. She leaned on him as he walked her to a chair. Her shoe was broken again! Todd and Chantelle approached Jennifer with sour faces and grim expressions. They each scolded her for the embarrassment of the situation. Jeff was disgusted by Todd and Chantelle's shocking behavior. How could they blame Jennifer for what had happened? Her informal dress was the result of an accident, and Bill alone was responsible for his behavior.

Jeff stood close behind Jennifer's chair to offer his support. "I've been dodging your perverted old man all evening. If anyone should be embarrassed, it's him." Jennifer exclaimed, pushing the bouquet at Chantelle. Then she turned to her brother. "How does any of this reflect on you? No one even knows we're connected. You ditched me as soon as we got here." Jeff glared at his friend. Then Jennifer turned back to Chantelle. "You should take this dance with your disgusting father. I think I sprained my ankle. I just want to go home."

When Todd glared at Jennifer and escorted Chantelle back to the dance floor, Jeff came around the chair and knelt down to check Jennifer's injured foot. "When did your brother get to be such a jerk?" he asked her.

He was floored by the shocked look on her face. "He's always been this way, and you've never been much better," she asserted. "I'm surprised you're not already getting your digs in. I'm really not looking forward to the drive home with him."

Jeff knew the time to discuss transportation had arrived. "About that, I'm your ride," he said. "Let me pack up my camera gear. Then, as soon as you're ready, we can go." He looked at her swollen ankle. "Can you walk?" Jennifer removed her broken shoes again and wobbled as she rose, testing her ankle. Jeff winced when she gasped in pain. "I think you better sit down again. I'll pack up my car and take you to the ER."

Jeff picked up his camera bag, folded his tripod, and found his gym bag. He shuffled out to his car and packed his gear into his trunk. He checked his front seat to make sure it was ready for company. Jeff grabbed a plastic bag and quickly collected the fast-food wrappers and other garbage that littered his passenger seat. Convinced his car would be acceptable to transport his guest, Jeff returned to Jennifer's chair, throwing his car trash bag into a large garbage can inside the reception venue.

Jeff asked Jennifer if she had a coat or other items he needed to collect before they could leave. She handed him her broken shoes, grabbed her purse and the bag with her wet dress in it, and hesitantly stood up, shaking her head to indicate that there was nothing else she was leaving behind. Jeff wrapped his arm around her waist and encouraged her to lean on him as she limped out to his car. With each step, Jennifer whimpered. Jeff knew her swollen ankle must be giving her a great deal of pain. He guided her to a bench just outside the door. Then he took her purse and bag to load into his car along with her shoes. Returning to the bench, he swept Jennifer up into his arms.

"Jeff!" She gasped. "Put me down! I'm way too heavy for you to carry like this!" But Jeff ignored her, striding to his car as though she weighed no more than a feather. He tucked her into the passenger's seat, closed her door, and settled himself behind the wheel. He glanced at Jennifer, making sure she was ok before he checked his mirrors to exit his parking space. He smiled at the beautiful blush covering her cheeks. Just then her stomach growled.

"Chantelle didn't put you off the wedding supper, did she?" Jeff inquired, remembering the plastic blonde's disdain.

"No. Todd ordered mushrooms on everything," Jennifer replied, softly. Jeff thought back to a summer vacation visit to the hospital where Jennifer had broken out in hives after Todd had slipped a mushroom onto her hamburger. Todd had been severely punished for endangering his sister, and Jeff had spent a good portion of that summer lonely. Spotting an open convenience store, Jeff pulled over.

"Wait here," he told Jennifer as he left the car to find her something to tide her over until he could feed her properly. Fifteen minutes later, he emerged from the store with a plastic bag full of snacks and two cups of coffee. He opened the passenger door, handed the bag and one of the cups to Jennifer, and returned to the driver's seat. "Two creams, two sugar," he said. "Is that still the way you take it? They didn't have a vanilla latte."

He noticed the surprise in Jennifer's eyes that he had remembered her coffee preferences. "Yes, that's just how I like it," she smiled at him.

She'd barely been old enough to drink coffee the last time he had seen her, but Todd had made a big deal out of teasing Jennifer about the "excess" of creamer in her coffee, and the memory had stuck with Jeff.

Traffic was light at this time of night. Jeff smoothly navigated the mostly empty streets between the convenience store and the hospital while Jennifer quietly munched on the snacks he bought her and sipped at her coffee, occasionally offering to share with him. He focused on the road, making sure to keep his driving smooth so as not to jar her injured ankle.

Arriving at the hospital's emergency entrance, Jeff parked the car and carried Jennifer inside to the waiting area. "You better let me give you my phone number, Jen," he insisted. "If they get you back there before I come back from parking, they might not let me come back to see you. You'll need to text me when you're ready for me to take you home." Jennifer unlocked her phone and passed it over to Jeff. He added himself to her contacts and then sent himself a quick text message so that he'd have her number too. Then he returned to his car to find a more appropriate parking spot, one not blocking the entrance.

Chapter Six - Jennifer

Jennifer filled out the ER intake forms, waiting for her turn to be seen. She looked around the nearly empty waiting room, wondering how long it would take for someone to see her. Her ankle throbbed as she filled in her paperwork. She was grateful that she still had her health insurance through the end of the month. Losing her job meant it would have been a really expensive trip to the hospital if her insurance didn't extend beyond today.

Jennifer passed the paperwork and her insurance card over to the receptionist and hobbled to a seat. A short wait later, a nurse popped into the waiting room, looked at Jennifer, and inquired, "Jennifer Jones?"

"That's me," Jennifer replied, struggling to her feet. She painfully followed the nurse back to be examined. It was a long and uneventful examination. Eventually, the nurse tucked Jennifer into a wheelchair and wheeled her back into the ER waiting room with the diagnosis of a sprain and a brace on her ankle. At the beginning of her visit, Jennifer texted Todd, but it was two hours later, and he still had not responded. Her stomach growled hangrily. She really needed to eat soon. Jennifer looked around the waiting room to see if Jeff was there. The room seemed empty.

Jennifer sent Jeff a quick text message.

[Jennifer: verdict: sprained ankle. They're sending me home]

Then she added:

[Jennifer: Todd is not responding. Can you give me a ride]

Within seconds she had a response. Jeff sent a gif of Captain America saluting. She saw headlights pull up in front of the ER entrance. The double doors slid smoothly open, and Jeff strode in, looking around for her. He grinned when he spotted her. "If it isn't the ravishing Jennifer Jones! Your chariot awaits," he declared. The nurse wheeled Jennifer out to Jeff's car, and Jeff once again lifted her and placed her in the passenger seat. The nurse returned inside, and Jeff closed the car door and slipped behind his steering wheel.

"Where should I take you, Jennifer Jones?" he asked. Jennifer's stomach loudly protested, and Jeff chuckled. Jennifer blushed, embarrassed once again. "It looks like an all-night drive-thru is our next stop," Jeff determined.

"That would be amazing," Jennifer gratefully murmured. "I'd eat anything, as long as it has no mushrooms on it."

Jeff drove along the main commercial road keeping an eye out for lights indicating an open restaurant. He pulled through a drive-thru at a popular fast-food place and ordered them each a cheeseburger with french fries and a milkshake. Jennifer was grateful when Jeff parked his car in the parking lot and parceled out the food. With the car parked, she didn't feel like she had to rush to eat. Self-consciously, she nibbled at her french fries.

"You've had quite the eventful day, Jen," Jeff asserted. Jennifer nodded at him and took a small bite of her burger.

"You have no idea," she replied, digging into her burger with gusto. "What you saw at the wedding was nothing compared to my morning." Jeff expressed his curiosity as he unwrapped his own burger and sipped his milkshake. Jennifer told him of the crane accident that had demolished her apartment.

"Really?" Jeff asked. "Bad luck always did follow you around. I've never known anyone else who could find herself in trouble as you can."

"I'm just lucky that way," Jennifer replied. "Todd will never let me live this down."

"He seems more uppity than he used to be," Jeff commented. "Todd used to have a sense of humor. Who spit in his cereal this morning?"

Jennifer grinned. She attributed Todd's high opinion of himself to his rapid promotions in his job. Jennifer always found Todd's work incredibly boring, but Todd seemed to relish the thrill of climbing the corporate ladder, and he'd found enough success to inflate his already substantial ego. Jennifer was quite proud of her brother, even if she dreaded relying on him in times of crisis.

"How did you get involved in wedding photography?" Jennifer asked Jeff. "Weren't you off to take over the world through coding?"

Jeff replied that indeed he had achieved a master's degree in computer science and that he worked at an IT company full time. Photography was his passion and hobby, and he'd only done this wedding as a favor to the bride's brother.

Their food finished, Jeff collected the wrappers and garbage and threw them in one of the parking lot's trash bins. Restarting the car engine, Jeff asked Jennifer, "So you're staying with Todd now?"

"That's the plan," Jennifer replied. "My apartment complex is unsafe until the construction crew fixes the damage caused by their crane." She checked her phone to see if Todd had responded to her text messages. He had sent nothing. Jennifer frowned. "This could be trouble," she told Jeff.

"More difficulty?" he asked.

"Todd hasn't responded, and I don't have a key to his apartment. I can't ask you to drive me four hours to my parent's place," she sighed. "Well," Jeff responded, "it looks like you're coming home with me. This could be the beginning of a beautiful friendship."

CHAPTER SEVEN – JEFF

Jeff pulled his car into his parking space and came around to open Jennifer's door. She insisted that she could hobble to the elevator. Jeff reluctantly agreed to let her walk but insisted she lean on him for support. Jennifer slumped against the elevator wall as they rode up to the third floor where Jeff's condo was located. Jeff watched the fatigue and embarrassment of the day wash across Jennifer's face until the elevator beeped and the door smoothly slid open. Jeff wrapped his arm around Jennifer's waist once again and guided her down the hall to his front door. He wondered what she would think of his modest bachelor pad. He watched her face as he opened the door and helped her inside.

Jeff was pleased when Jennifer smiled as she glanced around his great room. He had appreciated the open concept when he first viewed his condo, and it seemed she enjoyed the airy feeling of the space that housed his living, kitchen, and dining areas.

"This looks like a coder's paradise." Jennifer chuckled. "Is that your own private server?"

Jeff helped her to his cluttered couch, cleared a space for her to sit, and proudly showed off his electronics. "Yes, that's my server. I built it myself. I have it running NixOS!" Jeff pointed out his router, switches, and other networking equipment he enjoyed working with in his spare time. Jennifer seemed suitably impressed, asking questions about his network configuration that he hadn't expected. "Are you in IT?" he asked Jennifer. She replied that she was between jobs.

When he had completed the circuit of his electronic toys. He offered Jennifer a drink and his TV remote so she could settle in while he unpacked his car. He put away his camera equipment and pulled out the SD card from his camera to process the wedding videos. Then he showed Jennifer to his guest bedroom and offered her a towel and a change of clothes. He took Jennifer's damp dress, checked the label, and ran it through the "delicate" cycle on the washing machine.

It was extremely late, or very early, if you chose to look at it that way. Jeff had been on his feet for hours at the wedding and was exhausted. He texted Todd to see if he'd have better luck with a response than Jennifer and then got himself ready for bed. When there was no reply after half an hour, Jeff plugged in his phone to charge, moved Jennifer's dress to the dryer, shut off his bedside light, and settled in to sleep. As he drifted off, his thoughts turned to Jennifer and the circumstances that brought her close to him this evening. Exhausted, he slept soundly until his alarm woke him in the morning.

CHAPTER EIGHT - JENNIFER

Jennifer woke to the enticing aroma of coffee wafting through the air. She blinked, unsure where she was for a moment. Then the twinge in her ankle reminded her of the disastrous wedding reception the night before and the events afterward. Jennifer reached for her phone from where she'd left it on the nightstand, only to find it dead.

Jennifer sat up, removed the brace from her leg, grabbed the towel Jeff had provided the night before, and hobbled into the bathroom to get ready for the day. She was impressed by the array of hotel-sized bottles she found in Jeff's bathroom cupboards. She selected a shampoo, conditioner, and body wash that would suit her needs. Her ankle throbbing, Jennifer kept her shower relatively short. She found a new toothbrush in one of the bathroom drawers and was grateful to be able to clean her teeth. Her hair wrapped in the towel, Jennifer put on the clean clothes Jeff had provided. Then she returned to the bedroom and put the brace on her ankle. Ready to face the day, Jennifer hobbled into the great room, looking for Jeff.

She found him at his computer, sorting through photos from the wedding the day before. He grinned up at her from his seat and stood to help her to sit down on his couch.

"Do you need ice for that ankle, Jen?" he inquired.

"What I need most," she replied, "is a way to charge my cell phone. Do you think Todd is ok?" Jeff riffled through the cords near his computer and pulled out a charger cable with ends for three different types of phones.

"I bet Todd's phone battery died last night, and he is fine," Jeff averred. "Will this cord work?" Jennifer examined each of the three ends, finding one that would plug into her phone. She plugged the proper end in, then handed her phone and the cord to Jeff.

Jeff connected her phone to his computer's USB port to charge. Then he offered Jennifer a cup of coffee. Jennifer inhaled the fragrant steam from her cup, a look of bliss on her face.

"How are the wedding pictures coming?" she inquired.

Jeff turned his screen to show Jennifer the picture he was touching up. It was the photograph of herself with the bride after the bouquet toss. Her face colored, remembering her embarrassment at the attention she'd received while wearing his gym clothes. Jennifer watched as Jeff skillfully retouched the photo to disguise her clothing, making it seem more formal.

"Wow!" She breathed. "That's truly impressive, Jeff."

Jeff saved the retouched photo and closed down his photo editing software. "I'm ready for a break," he asserted. "How about some breakfast?" Jennifer agreed that breakfast sounded wonderful. Jeff offered to cook eggs, pancakes, bacon, or sausage or to provide her with cereal, but Jennifer insisted that a slice of toast and her coffee would be sufficient.

Over breakfast, they discussed plans for the day. "I really need to get in touch with Todd." Jennifer insisted. "I need to determine if I'm staying with him or need to find a way back to my folks' place until I find a new job." Jeff agreed to help her try to track Todd down. Frustrated at Todd's lack of response, each left voice mail messages requesting Todd call them back. Jennifer also called her parents, asking if either of them had heard from Todd. With nothing more to do to reach Todd, Jeff and Jennifer regrouped to determine how to spend the rest of the day.

"I'd hate to take you away from your photography work," Jennifer insisted. "If you can loan me a computer, I can update my resume and start applying for jobs again."

Jeff was happy to accommodate Jennifer. For the rest of the morning, Jeff retouched wedding photos while Jennifer submitted online job applications. Between applications, Jennifer checked her text messages to see if Todd had responded. There was nothing from him.

By late morning, Jennifer felt as though she had accomplished much, having submitted her resume, cover letter, and application to at least a dozen open positions. Feeling a little hungry, she hobbled to Jeff's kitchen to see if there was anything she could whip up for lunch. Impressed by Jeff's available fresh produce, Jennifer carefully prepared a couple of Cobb salads with sandwiches on the side. Then she called Jeff to lunch. They chatted about their morning accomplishments. Jennifer was pleased with her job search progress, and Jeff was frustrated with a problematic photo or two. Together, they cleaned up their lunch dishes, Jeff washing, and Jennifer drying.

"We make a good team," Jeff said. And Jennifer agreed.

Just then, Jennifer's phone squawked an email notification. Seeing the email was from one of the businesses she'd applied to, Jennifer sat down and held her breath while opening it. Then she let out a shriek of joy! She'd received a job offer from her favorite of the positions she'd applied to. She quickly emailed an acceptance of the offer and stood up to hobble a little happy dance.

"Good news?" Jeff inquired. Jennifer enthusiastically described her new position with a start date on Monday. Jeff hugged Jennifer, lifting her off the floor to swing her around in glee. "I'm so proud of you, Jen! We should celebrate! Let me take you out to dinner tonight!" Jennifer agreed.

"Thank you for loaning me your computer, Jeff," Jennifer exclaimed. "Without your kindness this weekend, I don't know where I'd be. You're so much nicer than you used to be." She hugged Jeff warmly. He squeezed her back, inquiring about the state of her ankle. When she admitted that it still throbbed, he insisted that she put her foot up with ice and entertain herself with his streaming services while he continued working on the wedding photos. Jennifer drifted off to sleep, binge-watching comedic science fiction shows.

Chapter Nine – Jeff

Jeff sighed as he finished touching up a particularly troublesome picture. The lighting in the church cast strange shadows on the faces of the bridal party, and Jeff had struggled to bring the appropriate romantic tone to the photo. After much manipulation, however, Jeff was pleased with the result. He hoped the bride would be pleased too. Jeff glanced away from his computer to the couch where Jennifer reclined, asleep, while the TV played quietly in the background. She truly was a lovely sight, even with a swollen ankle and borrowed clothing. Deciding to take a break, Jeff stood from his computer chair, stretched, and grabbed his phone.

Stepping out to his balcony to avoid waking Jennifer, Jeff dialed Todd's number once again. The phone rang a couple times, and then Todd finally answered.

"Dude, where have you been?" Jeff demanded of Todd. "Jennifer and I have been trying to reach you since late last night!"

Todd sighed. "You probably won't believe me. After you left, trouble found me just like it used to find Jennifer." Todd regaled Jeff with a story starting with a fight on the dance floor started by a very drunk Bill, ending with a trip to the county jail caused by Chantelle's erratic driving and the presence of illicit substances in her trunk. "Is my sister ok?" Todd asked.

"Her ankle is sprained," Jeff replied. "And she is exhausted from her traumatic day yesterday." Then Jeff chastised Todd for his poor treatment of his sister at the wedding reception. "I know we enjoyed teasing Jennifer when she was younger," Jeff said, "but I don't remember us being cruel to her. How could you treat her so badly? Your behavior was so unlike the Todd I grew up with."

Todd expressed his remorse. "I know I need to apologize to Jennifer," he said. "I got caught up in business and trying to impress Chantelle and forgot that Jennifer has never been comfortable in that kind of social setting. I have no excuses. I know I behaved badly. I'm sorry for the trouble it's caused you. Thank you for being a good friend to her when I let her down," Todd enthused.

"I'd like to be more than that," Jeff suggested. "Jennifer is lovely, funny, and smart. I really like her, Todd. I'd like to date her."

"If Jennifer wants to date you, it doesn't bother me," Todd agreed. "I always thought she had a crush on you when we were younger. She blushed more when you teased her than when I did, and she always wears that necklace you gave her at the county fair."

Jeff had a lot to think about. Assuming that Jennifer would want to share her job news with her brother herself, Jeff said nothing about it. Todd arranged to come to get Jennifer after he returned home to shower and change and bring her a spare key to his apartment so that she wouldn't be stranded again. Jeff returned to the great room to wake Jennifer.

The sound of the balcony sliding door closing caused Jennifer to stir in her sleep. Jeff walked over to the couch, leaned over, and kissed her on the forehead. "Wake up, sleeping beauty," he said. "Todd is on his way." Jennifer blinked up at him, slowly waking up.

"What?" She stretched. "You've heard from my brother?"

Jeff told her of Todd's disaster of an evening and then asked if there was anything she needed before her brother arrived. Jennifer yawned, considered his question, and asked for her dress from the wedding. Jeff retrieved the dress from the dryer. Jennifer hobbled to the guest room and changed back into her own clothes. Jeff straightened up the great room while waiting for her to return.

The doorbell rang. Jeff invited Todd inside. He seemed exhausted and downcast. Jeff knocked on the guestroom door. "Jennifer? Your brother is here," he told her. Jennifer limped out of the bedroom with her broken shoes and purse in hand.

"Have you seen my phone, Jeff?" she asked. Jeff retrieved her phone from the charger cord attached to his computer.

"What time should I pick you up this evening?" He asked her as he handed the phone back to her. "Would six work?"

Jennifer gazed into his eyes, determining if he was sincere in his desire to take her out. "Six will be fine," she replied. Jeff was pleased that she'd found what she was looking for in his eyes.

Todd offered Jennifer his arm as he escorted her out of Jeff's condominium. Jeff heard Todd apologize to Jennifer for the disaster of the night before. He was pleased to hear the siblings making up and hoped Todd would treat Jennifer better in the future. Jeff smiled. He had a date to prepare for this evening.

EPILOGUE - JENNIFER
Two Years Later

Jennifer clutched her boyfriend's arm as she tottered on her high heels across the floor of the restaurant where he'd first asked her to go out with him. Finding a bump in the carpet, she tripped, and the heel of her shoe broke, but Jeff kept her from falling over.

"This seems familiar, Jen." He smiled at her, bending to retrieve her broken heel, and helping her to keep her balance as they followed the hostess to their table.

Jennifer laughed. "I have the worst luck with shoes," she grinned. "It's fortunate that I have such good taste in men." Jeff and Jennifer ordered their drinks and appetizers and reminisced over the wedding that had brought them together. Jennifer had flourished in her new job and had moved back into her apartment once it had been repaired following the crane accident.

Jennifer's relationship with Todd had improved since she'd started dating Jeff. Todd had apologized profusely for his cruel behavior at the wedding, for the degrading comments, the mushroom gravy, and the lack of care and attention that he'd provided her. Then he'd made an effort to be supportive and encouraging of his sister as she started her new job and waited for her apartment to be repaired.

Todd's trip to the county jail had put him on probation at his job, but he had been more careful about the connections he developed and returned to good standing. Jennifer was proud of him for the way that he had matured. She encouraged her brother to rekindle his friendship with her boyfriend. Jeff and Todd developed a pattern of regular "guys" outings, hiking, and fishing together every few months. Yesterday, the two of them had disappeared for several hours.

The dinner conversation flowed smoothly. Jeff and Jennifer laughed and talked over the delicious food. After the server cleared away her plate, Jeff took her hand and dropped to one knee, holding out a small, velvet box.

"Jennifer, I know we haven't always been the best of friends but seeing you blush has always been one of my favorite things. I can't imagine my life without you in it. I love you. Please say you'll do me the honor of being my wife."

Jennifer blushed, smiled, and said, "Yes!"

MINE TO MAKE
Devon Borkowski

ISRA HADN'T THOUGHT THEY HAD ANY MUTUAL friends left. After college, most of *their* friends became *her* friends, and honestly, he'd never blamed them. The last holdout had been Jon, who'd initially introduced them, and then later blocked *both* their numbers when being the begrudging mediator started to feel more like nuclear disarmament.

And yet, there she was, picking apart her place card at table seven. Her curled bob hid her face from his vantage point, loitering by the door, but every time she turned his way, he became more sure. That profile would never stop being familiar. Be it cast in harsh fluorescent hallway lighting, catching her in the dorm stairwell at 2 a.m., or here, in the decadent elegance of a manor ballroom, three hours into the reception.

The rest of the table had gone to dance. He'd seen them out there on the ballroom floor— even taken her seat neighbor for a spin, all the while straining past the girl's shoulder, peering through the crowd. It poked something near his navel to see Beck sitting alone, a pang equal parts fond and sad. Isra was halfway across the room before he'd even made the decision to move.

"You got a haircut."

Beck set down the mangled remains of her manila nameplate and leaned back in her seat. Her eyes, when they met his, were smiling.

"I've had a few since we've last seen each other."

"Okay, smart ass. You know what I meant."

He set his hip against the table. The floral centerpiece teetered, and Beck reached to steady it. She tucked a curl behind her ear.

"I was a little tipsy, and I got a hold of the kitchen scissors," she said, brushing her fingers through the fringe at her jaw. "By the time anyone noticed, I'd already taken off a chunk near the front, so there wasn't anything anybody could do but help me even it out."

He laughed. "Well, it looks nice."

"I know." She propped her chin on her knuckles, elbows spread on the tabletop, "Are you going to sit down, or would you rather loom awkwardly for the rest of the night?"

"Who says I was to hang out with you the *rest of the night*?"

Beck leveled him a long, flat look. He sat down next to her, his suit trousers brushing her knee as he adjusted into the chair. Beck's dress was blue, like the bachelor's buttons tattooed over her clavicle, and low cut. A dainty silver chain dotted with pearls hung from her neck. It matched the one looped between her cuff and lobe piercing. She was beautiful, but he knew better than to tell her so.

"You don't seem surprised to see me."

She shrugged, "I saw you at the ceremony. Plus, I remember you were pretty close with Ashley back in the day."

"That I was. I didn't know you were, though."

"I wasn't. I'm here with the bride. Or— the *other* bride," She pointed to the happy couple where they spun on the dance floor. Sam had her arms around Ashley's neck, her eyes closed. She'd started crying at the altar, and it showed in her makeup, but she seemed far from bothered. "We've worked together for … nearly three years now. She's probably one of my favorite people, but you can never tell her I said so."

"For sure, Becky."

She scrunched her nose, "I can count on one finger the number of people who get away with calling me that."

"Which finger?"

He laughed as she flipped him off.

The DJ transitioned into another waltz. Couples smiled indulgently at each other around the room, settling in for the awkward embrace-and-sway. Beck picked up the place card to her left and started folding it along the lines of a paper plane.

"Wasn't Sam in our year too?"

Beck pressed her finger down over a crease, checking its sharp fold. "She was, but we didn't know her. She was a Bio major. Spent most of her time on the other side of campus. Turns out we did have a few mutual acquaintances, but I didn't even know that until we started hanging out outside of work."

"Small world."

"And getting smaller."

She smoothed a spot on the tablecloth and set her plane down beside an empty champagne flute. It tipped to the side, resting on one of its wings. Isra flicked it with his pointer finger.

"Twenty bucks says you could hit a bridesmaid from here."

Beck snorted, "You don't have twenty bucks."

"Shows how much faith I have in your aim."

She crossed her arms over her chest, "I'm not going to throw a paper airplane at a wedding. It's *beyond* inappropriate."

"Fine then," He snatched the plane from the tabletop and stood, "I'll do it."

"You will not!" Beck scrambled from her seat after him, grabbing for his hand. He held the plane just above where her grasping fingertips could brush. She scowled. Her eyes raked him over, clearly debating if it was beneath her dignity to jump.

"Mama didn't raise no bitch."

"No, she raised a fucking menace!"

Isra cocked his arm back, prepared to launch. Beck grabbed him by the wrist, her fingers in a bruising grip as she dragged his arm down. He jerked his arm, fingers closing instinctively in the struggle. Beck caught his hand in both of hers and pried the now-smashed plane from his hold.

She cupped her ruined creation in her palm. The wings were mangled, and there was a tear down the center crease. The nose was so snubbed; it was nearly inverted.

"Sorry, Becky. I was just kidding about throwing it."

Beck shrugged. She wadded the name card up and tossed it back on the table. "It was only a paper plane."

The DJ took to the microphone, calling "Let's get things moving up in here!" and the music switched to a club mix. Isra bopped his head to the song.

"Want to go dance?"

"You know that I don't." Beck's fingers curled around her skirt hem.

"Oh right, you've got your *thing* about dancing."

"It's not a *thing*," she sniped, her cheeks going red, "I just don't know what to do with my arms, and I always feel like my body is moving weirder than everyone else's somehow... It's just not fun for me, alright."

He'd only ever taken her to one house party, back in undergrad. They'd barely known each other at that point, friends-of-friends more than anything, but there was already such a magnetism about her. Her quick-witted conversation, and the way she'd bite the tip of her tongue when she smiled. He'd wanted to know her better. He invited her to the party in a near intoxicated moment of wanting to be near her.

She'd spent the entire event with her arms pinned at her sides, flighty rabbit eyes darting around for an exit. They left after only half an hour, and she threw up in the parking lot. It was a miracle they made it to a second date.

Isra shook the memory off and touched the toe of his shoe to her ankle, "You gotta learn to loosen up a little."

"I don't want to hear it from the guy who can't fucking slow dance," she said, scowling towards the dance floor. "Even *middle schoolers* have that one figured out."

"It's not that I can't—"

Beck raised her eyebrows, her face downright smug.

"Whatever. See if I try to give you advice next time."

"Oh no, wherever will I be without your unsolicited opinion." She turned her back to the dance floor and offered him her elbow, "Come on, let's go take advantage of the open bar tab."

He looped his arm through hers, "Ah yes, mooching off our friends' alcohol. The only good reason to go to a wedding."

The bar was to the back of the hall. A few uncles, cousins, and coworkers of the newlyweds mingled there, but no one Isra knew. Beck made a few polite hellos as they passed by but didn't seem inclined to stop for conversation.

"A Dirty Shirley and a Rum and Coke, please," Beck said, batting her eyes at the bartender. Isra leaned close to her ear.

"You know there are easier ways to get a strong drink."

She smirked. "Green is a bad color on you."

Beck knew how to do that. How to flirt just enough, and how to get away with it. She knew to be cutting and charming and how to teeter between the two. Up on a tightrope and making it look effortless, all the while waving to the poor suckers beneath her with nothing to do but watch her go. He'd been enraptured by that once. A part of him always would be. But it could get old sometimes, being with a girl who knows, with dead certainty, she's the best you'll ever get.

The bartender slid both glasses to Beck. She passed Isra the Rum and Coke. He sipped it through the straw and grimaced. The rum burned in the back of his nose.

"I remember you making these with Malibu."

Beck laughed, "Malibu and Diet Pepsi. Getting drunk shouldn't have to taste like booze."

"Right," he bumped his shoulder to hers, "obviously, it should taste like diabetes in a solo cup."

"Hey! It was *Diet* Pepsi. Diabetic friendly all the way."

The bar lighting had a soft purple tint to it, and half of Beck's face was cast in its glow. She hardly looked real. Isra couldn't stop himself from turning in towards her, brushing the backs of cold fingers to the notch of her wrist. She shivered but didn't pull away.

"You look good tonight."

"Just tonight?"

"Take the fucking compliment."

Beck snickered, swirling her straw through the dregs of her drink, "You look good too."

He scoffed, looking down at his rented suit. It was a little tight in the shoulders, and the lopsided tie peeked out past the jacket.

"Well, *now* who's not taking the fucking compliment."

He ran a hand down his lapel, "No, it's just—"

"You look fucking good, Is." She set her glass on the bar top and turned to face him fully. She caught his hand in one of hers and set to tweaking his collar. "I wouldn't have said it if I didn't think so."

Beck plucked at the tie knot, sliding the fabric free. Isra tilted his head back for easier access, painfully aware of her deft fingers working just below his Adam's apple. She brushed her pinky across his neck as the knot came undone— just light enough to have been accidental. He felt a puff of breath in the hollow of his throat before she pulled back. Beck kept one side of the tie in either hand, eyeing the length.

Isra bit his bottom lip, looking down the line of polyester towards her, "What are you doing?"

"Improving on *good*," she said, her eyes fixed firmly on her own hands.

She came in close again, folding the tie back over itself. Isra closed his eyes, lulled by the gentle— if *insistent*— tuggings. He focused on the feeling of her so near. Her steady workman's hands and the pine-and-mint smell of her hair. She clicked her tongue on the backs of her teeth as she adjusted the knot. Isra wondered if she knew how few people he'd allow this from. He suspected she did.

Beck reached around to his collar, arms looped behind his neck as she flipped it back over the tie band. She pulled back just enough to peer up at him, resting her hands a moment on his shoulders before she drew them back towards herself.

"Double Windsor," she said, patting his breast pocket, "helps with the length."

He blinked. "Right. Thank you."

"Anytime."

Beck grabbed for her drink again. She sucked on the straw. Ice cubes rattled in the bottom of the glass.

"Want another?"

"I shouldn't." She tucked a curl behind her ear. "I've had two already."

"I forgot how shit your tolerance is."

She huffed, coy and indignant all at once, but didn't argue with him. Couldn't, really. Not with the shared memories that hung between them. Rubbing her shoulders through bouts of vomiting and then nursing her through the next morning's hangover.

"No one wants to be the person throwing up in the corner when it's time to cut the cake."

"I'd hold your hair back," he said, fighting a smile as he bumped their feet together.

"Oh yeah?" Beck leaned back on the bar and clicked her toes back against his.

"For sure. I'll find you a trash can and everything."

"What a gentleman."

"Yeah. And if you ask really nicely, I might even pull the Pedialyte out of my car."

"Well, that's almost *too* nice."

She tipped her head to the side and bit the corner of her mouth. He couldn't help it—the way a grin broke over his face.

"I know. So don't be saying I never gave you nothing."

"This is all, of course, conditional on me drinking enough to puke."

Beck pinched the end of the straw between her teeth, staring him down with her eyebrows raised. Isra could never refuse a challenge. He hailed the bartender over.

Two drinks later, Beck was tucked into his shoulder, her shoes dangling by their back strap over her pointer finger as she stumbled through a story from their senior year. She gestured wildly with her hands, and Isra had to bob out the way a few times to dodge a heel to the eye.

"—and then you, *you*," she slurred, "you fucking tossed me in the river!"

"Lies and slander," he said, hiding a smile in the crown of her hair.

"Is *not!*" She threw her hands out. The shoes swung to the side, nearly knocking a glass over. "You dickwad! You, you fucking— *menace!*"

Isra wrapped his arms around her, trapping her hands two his chest. Her shoes were digging into his armpit, but the bartender stopped shooting them a side eye once Beck was a little better contained.

"Yup, that's me."

Beck hitched her chin on his collarbone. She was too close to see properly. His eyes hurt trying to look at her on an angle. Still, like always with her, it was hard to look away.

It would be so easy to bend down and taste the Shirley Temple on her breath. She wouldn't object. He was sure. He'd wake up hating himself, but it might pair well with the hangover.

"Oh my god, Isra?"

His head snapped up. One of Sam's bridesmaids was squinting at him, her hand shading the purple light from her eyes.

"That is you, right?" She said, coming closer. Beck wriggled around in his arms, searching for the source of the disruption. "Oh my god, *and* Beck? How crazy to see you two!"

Isra studied the girl hard. Her dress was the same peachy pink as all the other bridesmaids. It paired well with her strawberry blonde curls. She had a slim, pale face and pointed chin. He couldn't have picked her out from a lineup.

Beck, on the other hand, huffed. "Hi, Maddy."

If *Maddy* heard, she didn't show it. She beamed at Isra. "It's been way too long!"

"Right," he tried to will the stiffness from his smile, "way too long."

Beck, tactless and tipsy as she was, laughed.

"Maddy lived in our dorm sophomore year. In case you forgot."

He had. And honestly, even knowing that he might have once known her, her face was still a stranger.

"Right, Maddy! Of course. Second floor?"

"First, actually."

"Right. Right."

Beck laughed again, and Isra jostled her a bit between his arms to quiet her. Maddy's smile grew a little stained.

"I didn't know you two were still together."

"Oh, we're not," Beck said cheerfully. "He dumped me. Right after graduation. Surprised you didn't hear."

Isra groaned and dropped his forehead into her hair. He was half impressed with how quickly this interaction had started to devolve. Beck was lounging back against him, loose and pleased with herself.

He'd never really thought of her as being cruel, but she certainly liked a little drama, and after a drink or two, it didn't much matter that her fun was coming at someone else's expense.

"Oh, I'm so sorry. I just assumed."

Maddy was flustered now, thin fingers fluttering about the neck of her champagne flute. Her eyes flicked around the room for an easy escape. Isra didn't blame her. He would've loved to make an excuse and go.

"Great to see you, Maddy," he said, aiming for charitable. "You're right. It's been way too long."

She nodded, then slipped back into the crowd. All poise and polite, wounded dignity. Isra watched across the room, through the bobbing heads of milling guests, as she tucked herself back into the gaggle of bridesmaids. The few scandalized glances cast in their direction were probably well deserved.

Beck dug a finger into his side, "Are you pissed with me?"

"Why would I be pissed with you?"

"Don't play stupid."

Her brows were raised, a thin press smirk on her lips. There was something hesitant flitting just behind her expression, though. A wavering uncertainty on where the line was and whether or not she'd crossed it. She squinted up at him, the slow, alcohol-soaked gears in her head turning.

"Honestly, I probably should be. You didn't have to do that."

"Do what?"

"Now who's playing stupid."

Beck pulled out of his arms. For a moment, she teetered, and he wanted to reach out and steady her, but she caught herself against the bar counter and leaned back into it. Something about the foot of space between them felt uncrossable now that she'd established it. Like she'd retreated to somewhere far away.

"Whatever. It's not like you even remember the bitch. Why do you care?"

"Maddy's not a bitch." Probably. At least, she hadn't seemed like one.

Beck snorted, "How would you know?"

"What do you actually have against her?"

He genuinely wanted to know. Beck could be a bit sharp, for sure, but rarely without cause to be. It had been a few years since they'd seen each other, sure, but he didn't want to think the core of her was so changed.

Beck picked at her cuticles. Her nail polish was dark grey and metallic, and starting to chip along the beds. She was quiet for so long that he started to give up on an answer. Then she sighed and pushed her hair back from her face.

"Maddy had a crush on you, did you know?" The words were airy and unaffected. He almost might've believed she wasn't even answering his question at all, if not for the way her mouth puckered all lemon-like. "The whole time we dormed together. Probably after that too. I don't know. I stopped paying any attention to her once she didn't live right down the hall."

Isra's first reaction was, of course, shock. He wasn't sure what exactly he did to inspire feelings in a girl he couldn't remember having spoken to before. The shock was quickly followed by a swirl of curiosity. He reconsidered her in his mind's eye, the pleasing bounce of her curls and the hug of her gown to her figure. He wondered if he would've been interested had she made her feelings more apparent.

Some of his musings must've shown in his look because Beck's face soured.

"In case it slipped your mind," she said, "we were already dating by the time you two met."

It surprised him that she would be so affected by another girl's attention, though maybe it shouldn't have. Jealousy was, after all, only human. Beck had always just seemed above all that somehow, so feckless and certain. Isra tried to meet her eyes, but she angled her head away. He watched the muscles of her jaw bunch, just short of grinding her teeth.

"You still didn't need to be a dick to her, Becky."

Beck lifted her chin up, took a deep breath, and held it. She looked braced for a fight, shoulders squared and eyes narrow. For a moment, he wasn't looking at her in the purple bar lighting. He was looking at Becky, his Becky, four years younger and standing on the steps of the Student Center, her long hair frizzy from the rain. She hadn't cried in front of him the day he ended things. Said she wouldn't give him the satisfaction. As if seeing her unhappy had ever done anything but break his heart.

"Well," she said, her voice cold and even. She still wouldn't look at him. "Why don't you go make it up to her then? I'm sure she'd appreciate it."

She marched back towards the dance floor. He watched her heels swing from her hand until she was gone.

He looked for her afterward. Just—he assured himself—to make sure she was okay. He started with the men's room, then when that proved fruitless, he sheepishly approached the girl next in line for the women's and asked that if she happened to see someone with a bob cut and a blue dress puking her guts out in one of the stalls, please let him know.

Several awkward moments loitering outside the bathroom later, no dice on that front either.

He scanned the ballroom for her a few times, almost against his better judgement. It didn't matter. She wasn't there.

When Sam's father, a jovial, red-faced man more than a few glasses of champagne in, called for the cutting of the cake most of the assembled guests started making their way towards the wedding party, the brides artfully arranged on either side of an artful, tiered confection.

Isra stayed at his table. His tie was undone and hanging off the back of his neck, and he put his forehead down on the table. It was a nice tablecloth at least. Soft. At least he had that to be thankful for.

"I'd ask if you were alright," said a voice from over his left shoulder, "but I'm not really sure you deserve to be."

Isra jolted up. Maddy was bent at the waist, hands locked behind her back. Her bottom lip was pinched between her teeth, but she looked more tired than teasing.

"Hi- I... Yeah," he pushed his thumbs into the corners of his eyes, "that's probably fair."

"Yeah. It is."

She slid into the seat next to him and brushed her curls back over her shoulder.

"Shouldn't you be up there getting cake?" All the other bridesmaids were. One gaggle of peach and another in lavender.

"I probably should be," she said. "Everyone over there actually remembers my name."

"Ha, yeah ... that's, for sure, a point in cake's favor."

"You seriously don't remember me at all."

He searched her face. It was pale, angular, pretty, and utterly unfamiliar.

"I'm really sorry."

"God," she laughed, "I was so stupid over you!"

Isra found that really hard to imagine. Maddy was pretty, albeit forgettably so. And a good sport, too, if the fact that she was keeping him company was any indication.

"In my defense, I was seeing someone at the time."

She eyed the half-empty flute of champagne on the table in front of her. She picked it up and swirled it with a flick of her wrist, cautiously sniffing it a few times before taking a sip.

"Oh, believe me, I know." She traced the flutes brim with her finger, "I was always so jealous of Beck, you know? Not just because of you. She just … she was so mean all the time, and everybody liked her anyway. I never saw her study, but she never seemed to fail. It all just kinda worked out for her, even though she didn't seem to give a shit. Like she wasn't even trying. Do you get what I mean?"

He did. He remembered thinking the same thing, once, of the pretty girl who marched over to his table in the dining hall— a two-seater near the back, where people went to eat alone— and sat her plate down across from him. She'd had on a sundress and Timbs, with her hair in a braid over her shoulder. She sat down and said, "You live in my dorm, and I hate eating alone." And in that moment, she'd seemed bulletproof. Like Superman but with better tits. Untouchable in the ways that normal people are just not.

He also remembered, though, the girl who called him at two in the morning, sobbing over the phone only three days into winter break because she was convinced all her hometown friends secretly hated her. The girl who apologized after their first date for not being "fun at parties" the way that "normal people can be." Honestly, he realized with a pang, it shouldn't have surprised him that Beck was just as jealous of Maddy as Maddy was of her. Beck hid her insecurities well, but he knew better than most that didn't mean they weren't there.

He thought about saying this to Maddy— It would probably make her feel better at the very least— but in the end, he knew where his loyalties lay. Maddy seemed like a sweet girl, but he'd made Beck promises. Her secrets weren't his to share.

"Yeah," he settled on eventually, "I do get what you mean."

Maddy drowned the rest of her borrowed drink and then stood, smoothing her dress as she did.

"Well, I think I am going to join the cake cutters," she said, looking over to where Sam had just smeared a dollop of frosting on Ashley's nose in lieu of the whole cake-face tradition. Maddy paused before leaving. She dropped a hand to his shoulder. "I happened to see Beck sneaking out towards the terrace. If that fact at all interests you."

Isra thought about pretending not to know what she meant but decided he'd already insulted her enough for one evening.

The sound of crickets in the cool night air was such a stark contrast to the lights and music of the ballroom it nearly took his breath away. He shut the door behind him as quietly as he could, trying not to feel like an intruder.

Beck was poised against a filigree railing, her back towards the door. Her heels had been abandoned over on one of the glass table tops, one bare foot hooked behind the opposing ankle. Every so often, a stream of smoke would drift off her and up towards the purpling sky.

He went over and leaned on the railing next to her, his suit jacket brushing her bare arm.

"Can I get a hit?"

She pressed the pen into his hand, "It's strong."

"I'll be fine."

He took the pull, inhaled, and breathed it out in a fit of coughs. Beck left the *I told you so* implied in her hastily suppressed smile.

"I'm sorry," he said, once he could talk without choking again, "for picking a fight earlier."

"That wasn't really what I was upset about." She took the pen from him and hit it, whistling smoke out through painted lips before passing it back. "And for what it's worth, I'm sorry too."

They stood out there, fingers brushing as they passed the pen back and forth. The air grew colder as the last glimpse of sunlight faded away. Beck started to shiver, her shoulders prickling with goose bumps, and eventually, Isra shucked his jacket to drape it around her. She didn't thank him, but she leaned against him ever so slightly, sliding her arms into the sleeves.

Isra thought about Ashley and Sam. The way they'd looked during their first dances and married women, so wrapped up in each other that the rest of the party might as well have been another planet, or a grouping of far-off twinkling stars. He thought about how much it must've taken to get there. How brave they had to be to get through all the fights and curses and crying. To stand up at an altar in front of everyone who'd ever mattered to them and say, *"It's this one. Forever and ever, I'm sure, it's this."* Isra wasn't sure he'd ever be that brave. But oh, how he wished he was.

"What were you actually upset about, then?" He asked after far too long.

Beck buried her hands in the pockets of his jacket. She rocked on the balls of her feet. For a moment, he worried she might just go back inside and find some other way to disappear, but instead, she met his eyes.

"You told Jon you never loved me."

Isra's stomach dropped.

"What?"

"After the breakup. Back when Jon would still talk to either of us." She leveled a stare up through her lashes, "You do remember Jon, don't you?"

"Of *course*, I— "

"Just checking!" She tipped forward to lean on the railing again but kept watching him out the corner of her eye. "Anyway, that's why Jon finally stopped talking to me in the end, I think. I kinda freaked out when he told me. I was going on and on about how I thought … well." She laughed, though the sound was less amused and more sardonically self-deprecating, "It doesn't matter what I thought. But he told me just to shut me up. That you didn't think you ever really loved me. Just loved the idea of loving me. Something to that effect, anyway. You'd know better than me."

Honestly, no, he probably wouldn't. He must have been near blackout drunk saying it, and it had been so long ago. His toes curled with the shame of it all.

"Beck ... I'm *so* sorry."

She shrugged, "I'm a big girl, Is. I got over it."

"I didn't mean— "

"I don't care." She said it firmly but not unkind. "It won't ... look, I've already done all the crying I can possibly do over this. You trying to explain it now would just be... There's no point, alright?"

"But I really didn't—"

"Is." She took him by the elbows, "It's over— it's *been* over. We don't need to do this whole song and dance again."

He wanted to fight her on it. He wanted to tell her he didn't mean it and that he never had. That if he could go back and erase all the hurt and tears, he would. But Beck wasn't crying now. She slid her hands from his elbows down to his wrists. Her eyes were bright, catching the yellow ballroom light where it spilled out the glass double doors. Faintly he could hear music just below the cricket calls and the occasional chirp of frogs. Isra let his arms sway, Beck still holding tight to his wrists.

"Dance with me."

She scoffed, "Haven't we had this talk before?"

"No, I ... I didn't mean *that* way."

He gently dislodged her grip around his wrists. For a moment, he wasn't quite sure where to go from there, his palms were starting to sweat, but with twitchy movements, he guided one of her arms up around his shoulders, then took her other hand and interlaced their fingers.

Beck raised a brow. She pressed her lips together. A smile broke over her face like a new day. He felt silly for ever having refused this. Who cared about looking stupid when it won him that smile?

"...I have no idea where my other hand is supposed to go."

"My hip," she said, and he complied. His thumb brushed the divet of her waist.

"What's next?"

Beck pressed in close, so close it almost hurt to look down at her, though he wouldn't dream of looking away.

"You just sorta sway," she said, resting her head against his chest. "Nothing too fancy."

He shuffled his feet back and forth, and she followed. They probably looked silly, but there was no one outside to care.

"This is easier than I thought it would be."

"Don't tempt me into saying I told you so."

They swayed and stepped, occasionally bumping feet. Luckily, Beck stepped on his shoes more often than the other way around, her bare toes just dimpling the leather. The crickets chirped on around them, their own little string band. Beck wound her fingers through the fringe of hair at his nape. Isra pressed his mouth into the crown of her head.

"What are we doing here, Becky?"

"Dancing."

He breathed her in, that pine-and-mint smell. Tried to memorize it, just in case he never got the chance again.

"No, I mean ... is there a chance ... is there anything left here to fix?"

She pulled back just enough to look him in the eyes. He wondered what she was thinking about. Malibu Rum and Cokes, the night he left her standing in the rain, the first time she met his parents, or her crumpled paper airplane left wadded up on the table. He couldn't find an answer in her eyes. She ducked back into his chest again.

"I don't know. Maybe not. Probably not, even. There's been a lot of hurt on both sides, Is, that doesn't just go away. But right now, I really don't care."

She held their interlaced fingers aloft and ducked herself under their clasped hands in a clumsy spin.

"Just dance with me, please?" she asked. And, even if it didn't change anything, even if it was just for this one night, he did.

Set Alight

Bevanny Stearman

THE SUN SHINES IN MY EYES AS I TURN MY car into the parking lot and quickly pull into an open space. A light breeze blows my hair around as I get out and walk towards the back entrance of the barn, and I notice there are just a handful of clouds decorating the sky. The temperature is cool for late September, but the sun warms my skin. It truly is a beautiful day for a wedding.

The old barn in front of me, renovated to become a wedding venue, is absolutely picturesque. A small lake sits just behind it, and further back, a smaller barn houses a half dozen horses. Open fields stretch out on all sides of the barn, turning into hills after a certain distance.

A few of my friends greet me as I enter through the back of the kitchen. After punching in, I make my way to the bathroom, where I pull my hair back into a high ponytail and quickly get dressed for the wedding. My plain black clothing is casual today, and I couldn't be more grateful for the added comfort it brings compared to my usual wedding attire. The final touch is the black apron I tie tightly around my waist, marked with the venue's logo that reads "Westwood Blue Barn."

My favorite coworker, Amber, is already in the dish room when I walk in. Unlike me, she's dressed for the guests. Her black slacks and matching button-down shirt fit her well, though she's struggling to tie her pale blue tie around her neck. I don't envy her; I'm long overdue for a comparatively relaxed shift doing dishes.

"Finally! I've been fighting with this thing for like twenty minutes!" Amber exclaims when she sees me.

"I saw you walking through the parking lot when I was pulling in. It's been two minutes at best," I chuckle as I help her out.

"Well, it felt like a lifetime," she remarks with a playful eye roll.

"Oh, shush. There you go." I straighten her tie and step back. "Gorgeous."

We turn toward the whiteboard, reading through the tasks our supervisor wrote for us to complete. The guests are scheduled to arrive at 2:30, so we have a couple of hours to clean the decks, organize the cookies for the cookie table, and set the tables in the reception space upstairs. Given today's lovely weather, the ceremony will take place outside at the gazebo.

"Ugh, do we really have to sweep the top deck?" Amber groans.

"Hey, it could be worse! At least we aren't Jacob," I reply, pointing out that Jacob was assigned to restocking the restrooms and setting up the decorations for the ceremony. It's always such a battle to decorate the gazebo, and it'll be even worse if that breeze picks up speed.

Just as the words leave my mouth, Jacob comes strolling in. Amber and I grin at him as he reads the whiteboard, laughing at his disgusted face when he reaches his assigned tasks.

"If I fall into the lake chasing after a bouquet of flowers again…" he grumbles.

"One of us will be there to fish you out. After we let you suffer for a few minutes, of course," Amber teases.

"Very funny. Maybe I'll pull you down with me this time," he pokes her a few times in the stomach, to which she responds by swatting wildly at him.

"You brat! Stop! You know I'm ticklish!" she squeals.

"Oops, guess I forgot," he shrugs with a grin, running out of the dish room before Amber can chase him out. She shakes her head at him as he disappears from sight, turning her attention back to me and our to-do list.

"Is there any chance you'd take care of all of this while I take a nap in The Dungeon?" she asks, referencing the tiny closet connected to the dish room, separated from the rest of the space with an old shower curtain. It's always jam-packed full of random little odds and ends. Emergency supplies to get us through our shifts, decorations left behind from past weddings, and vintage walkie-talkies that barely function are just the tip of the iceberg.

"Hmm..." I pretend to consider this. "You want me to do the work of two people while you get to kick back and relax? Yeah, no way."

"Ugh," Amber sighs. "Well, maybe if we finish up early, we can take a little break!" she adds. I expect her motivation to last all of 20 minutes.

We grab some supplies and head up to the top deck, where, 18 minutes later, Amber collapses into a chair. We're nearly done sweeping the top deck, but we still have all of the lower decks, plus our other tasks.

"Come on. We got this!" I try to encourage her as I swat away a massive bumblebee. "We'll be done before you know it."

She gives me a disbelieving look before throwing her head back and letting out an overdramatic groan.

"Iris?" she calls out to me as I start to walk away.

"Yeah?"

"Would you like to make me the happiest woman in the world?" I'm not looking at her, but I can picture the puppy-dog look she's undoubtedly putting on.

"That depends," I hesitate.

"You know, you're always so good with the guests! And I'm already exhausted, so how the heck am I supposed to be all polite and crap?" She gestures to herself. "Do I really look like a good representation of Westwood?"

I think I know where this is going, and I don't think I like it.

"I think it's really in everyone's best interest if we swap roles for the day," Amber finally says what I've been dreading.

Just the thought of interacting with guests today drains me of the excitement I felt earlier. Working in the dish room is my favorite and for good reason. The dish room may be a little bit gross, but we get to wear essentially whatever we want, remain unseen by guests, and get first dibs on whatever extras our chefs make. Plus, some of the most fun people work in the dish room regularly, and I could use a good laugh.

But I can't say no to Amber, even though I really, really want to.

"Fine," I concede, "but I hope you know that I didn't bring my dress clothes."

"You can have mine!" comes her quick offer. She hops to her feet and practically drags me to the bathroom with her.

Her clothes are a little bit tight on me, but we make it work.

Less than five minutes later, we're back to work. It's incredible how this little switch-up has given her mood a complete turnaround; Amber's now speeding through our tasks. She might even be working faster than me, which I don't think has ever happened.

Sure, she sneaks a cookie every few minutes for fuel while we set up the cookie table, and she disappears for a little while to find us some rolls to snack on, but those distractions are typical for her.

If she keeps working at this speed, it just might be worth suffering through a shift working the reception. Besides, how awful could it be?

I straighten my tie as I wait for the first round of guests to arrive. The bride and groom live a few towns over, but most of the guests have had to travel quite a bit to make it.

The nearby hotel is sending over three different shuttles of guests, and the remaining guests are driving themselves. In fact, with the exception of the bridal party, I think just about every guest is arriving on the shuttles. At least it will be a relatively small wedding.

A quick peek at my cell phone tells me that it's 2:26 PM. The guests should begin arriving at any minute now.

The front porch, where I'm waiting to greet the guests, receives the most sunlight in the afternoon. I have to squint as I look out towards the road for the first shuttle, which comes barreling noisily down the adjacent backroad a few moments later.

I press a button on my earpiece to speak into it. "First shuttle is pulling in now," I inform everyone.

Okay, I can do this. I've greeted thousands of guests at this point, maybe even tens of thousands. Today's crowd should be no big deal for me, so why is my stomach doing backflips?

The shuttle screeches to a halt in the driveway, and a mess of people flood out the doors as soon as they open—20-30 people come stampeding towards me.

"Welcome to Westwood Blue Barn!" I say cheerily as they get close. I open the main door and offer my most approachable smile. "While you wait for the outdoor ceremony to begin, please head down the stairs to the left for light refreshments. You'll find the card box at the bottom of the stairs and restrooms to the right from there."

I repeat this a few times as the crowd slowly makes its way past me. Most people smile back at me and nod, while a couple others ask me random questions. Still, about a third of the guests don't even acknowledge me and, instead, barrel past me with upturned noses. I can't help but hope they get lost in there.

I only spot a couple of the classic already-too-drunk guys who give me a little whistle or throw a line at me. Better than telling me to smile more, at least.

I take a quick breather as the last guests from the first shuttle wander down the stairs. Okay, one down, only two to go!

The second shuttle arrives a little more than five minutes later. I hold the door open as they come towards me, and I'm about to launch into my little spiel when I notice the groomsmen out of the corner of my eye. Rather, I notice one particular groomsman who I previously half-hoped I'd never see again.

Alex. His bright eyes are crinkled in laughter as he slaps one of the other groomsmen on the shoulder. He's grown a bit of a beard since the last time I've seen him, and he towers over the other four men dressed in navy suits. I can just barely hear his laugh as I watch the group happily stroll through the yard, quickly moving out of sight.

I'm so caught off guard that I almost forget about the herd of guests walking across the porch. I stumble over my words a little as I direct them, mentally blaming it on him. Once they're all inside, I use the few minutes between now and the last shuttle's arrival to get myself together.

No need to panic. So what if I haven't seen Alex since our high school graduation? Who cares if he was a complete jerk to me and abandoned our plans on our senior class trip? It's been just over five years, so surely I can act normal around him, right?

I'm not sure I want to find out.

My goal for today was originally to secure a box of peanut butter blossoms to take home with me at the end of my shift, but I'm now establishing a second, somewhat more important goal: Avoid Alex Thompson.

"No way!" Amber squeals after I fill her in on Alex. "Wait, come on, you have to show me which one he is. This is our best chance." She grabs my hand and pulls me out onto the back deck. We have a perfect view of the ceremony from here, which began just a few minutes ago.

"There." I point out towards the gazebo. "He's the tallest groomsman."

She squints and inches forward to get a better look at him. "Oh my gosh, Iris!" she exclaims. "He's absolutely gorgeous!"

I shush her, paranoid he'll somehow hear her from his place next to the groom.

Amber pulls a handful of pretzels out of her apron pocket and munches on them as she continues to stare at him. "I think you should go for it."

"Excuse me? Did you not hear me tell you about how he completely pushed me aside for someone else?" I ask in disbelief.

"Yes, but I also heard you say that it was half a decade ago! And you clearly still have some sort of feelings for him if you still care about his 'betrayal' anyway."

"I absolutely do not!" I protest without hesitation.

No. There is no way I have any positive feelings towards that boy. As I stare, I realize that perhaps 'boy' isn't fitting anymore -- not with that facial hair and those broad shoulders and...

Okay, enough of that. Sure, he's objectively handsome. That doesn't mean anything. Of course, Amber only chuckles at me as I express this to her. I just roll my eyes and head back inside.

The ceremony will be over soon and that means cocktail hour will be starting. I usually dread walking around the crowded space with platters of hors d'oeuvres, but I'm actually looking forward to it just this once. The bridal party takes professional pictures during cocktail hour while the guests all eat and drink. In other words, no Alex.

Carrie, our supervisor, sends me out into the mob of hungry, well-dressed pigs with a tray of stuffed mushrooms. They disappear in seconds, and I quickly go back for another tray. I'm on my sixth tray when Leonard, one of our new part-time workers, approaches me. I remember seeing his name next to the "Manage refreshments for bridal party during photography session" task on the whiteboard.

"Iris, I need you to come with me to the gazebo! The bridesmaids wanted a bottle of wine, but I'm too young to handle it," he says, reminding me he's only seventeen.

I suppose I have no choice but to help him. Lovely.

"Okay, let's get it done."

He points out the wine they wanted, and I grab two chilled bottles. I also pick up a corkscrew and a small tray of wine glasses, which I eventually let Leonard carry so that I don't drop the whole thing. It's bad enough that I'm about to come face to face with Alex, but it would be even worse if I made a total fool out of myself in front of him while I'm at it.

Leonard carries a pitcher of ice water, too. I'm assuming they emptied the first pitcher rather quickly, despite the cool temperature. In the direct sunlight, simply carrying the wine and corkscrew up to the top deck is enough for me to break a sweat.

The groomsmen are milling around the table full of snacks when we approach, and the bridesmaids are huddled around the bride as the photographer barks instructions at them.

As if sensing me, Alex lifts his eyes and looks directly at me.

His eyebrows pop up in recognition, and a second later, a wide grin spreads across his face. "Iris," his smooth voice greets me as Leonard and I get closer. Leonard shoots me a questioning look.

"Oh, hi Alex!" I pretend this is the first time I noticed his presence today.

He walks around the table to stand beside me as Leonard and I set up the drinks. "Wow, I haven't seen you in so long! Look at you," his eyes sweep over me. I, on the other hand, avoid eye contact.

"Time sure does fly," I remark neutrally as I struggle to uncork the second bottle of wine, probably due to my damp palms.

"Here, let me," he puts his hand on my arm, and my eyes shoot up to his in alarm. I instinctively step away, and he seems a little taken aback by my reaction.

"Oh, uh, that's okay. I got it," I look at Leonard and nod at him to come help me. He gets the cork out in no time.

Alex's face turns apologetic. "Listen…"

Oh God, no. Please stop. Anything but this.

"I know I wasn't exactly—"

"Alex!" the groom shouts, grabbing our attention. "Come on. We're up again."

Before he can turn back to me, I whip around and speed walk towards the stairs, noticing Leonard struggling to keep up in my peripheral vision.

Even if I did want to hear whatever poor excuse he could come up with for dropping the plans that *he* made with *me* to hang out with my best friend at the time, it wouldn't change anything.

I peek my head out from the kitchenette connected to the reception area. Yup, Alex is still staring in my direction, just like he has been ever since he saw me disappear back here the first time.

Why does he have to be seated facing me?

I scan the other tables while I'm looking, noticing that table seven's water pitcher is almost empty.

I dart back behind the little curtain separating me from the reception and pull down a pitcher from the cupboard. The bag of ice in the sink is still frozen solid, so I frantically bang it against the side of the counter to loosen it. I'm thankful that the chatter out there covers up the sound.

Somewhere along the line, I start thinking of Alex again.

I can still picture him pressed up against my best friend that night. I remember feeling like I was in a nightmare and that surely it wasn't really him. I thought there was no way it was real, especially after everything that had been said between us just hours before.

But it was real, and I was crushed.

"Hey, Iris, I notice table seven is running low on—" Katina walks into the kitchenette, stopping abruptly when she sees me.

I pause, feeling the sweat beading on my forehead; I must look like a crazy person attempting to murder this bag of ice. My face feels hot, and I see strands of hair breaking free from my ponytail in rebellious curls.

"What did that ice ever do to you?" Katina asks, a mixture of amused and concerned.

"Oh, I was just breaking it up a little more," I assure her as I busy myself filling a new pitcher. I quickly smooth my hair down, grab the pitcher, and turn to leave the tiny room without another word.

Of course, I'm instantly met with Alex's eyes. He watches me steadily, which only adds to my embarrassment. I keep my eyes focused on table seven, and after wiggling around a dozen guests unwilling to scooch their chairs in, I make it.

I quickly replace the pitcher with a smile, making note of a few other tables that will need more water soon. I get three more pitchers ready and waste no time in swapping them out for the old ones. I have to keep myself busy; I don't want to even think about...

Alex gives me a little wave and gestures to his table's empty water pitcher, which is conveniently sitting directly in front of him. It sits right beside his nearly overflowing glass of water, which he begins gulping down with a grin. I turn away, wondering how bad it would be if I refused to replace their pitcher.

That would be damaging enough if they were regular guests, but the bridal party? Yeah, those probably are not the people I'd want to be rude to today.

I fill up a new pitcher as full as I can while still avoiding the danger of a major spill, and I delicately carry it to the bridal party table. I warily reach around Alex for the empty pitcher, hoping to get this over with quickly. I can't let myself get distracted by him again.

"So, you come here often?" he asks, throwing a corny smile my way. I'm so caught off guard that I let out the slightest laugh, but I quickly hide any trace of a smile.

"How charming. Do you use that line often?" I counter.

"First time, actually."

"Hopefully, the last," I mutter, setting the very full pitcher down in front of him and briskly walking away.

Not even half an hour later, his table's pitcher is empty again. I shake my head, noticing that a few tables haven't even touched their first pitcher. Still, I prepare a new pitcher and approach his table, where he is staring at me expectantly.

"We can't keep meeting like this," he says lightly. When I don't respond, his tone shifts. I can feel his gaze locked on my face. "Look, Iris, I'd really like to talk to you. Alone. Preferably as soon as possible."

"I'm very sorry, Alex, but I don't exactly have time for that." I start to turn back to the kitchenette, but he reaches for my arm. The contact sends a shockwave through me, and it's not entirely unpleasant. That's what catches me off guard.

"Please?" he asks.

I'm trying to think, but his hand is still touching my arm, and I'm just now becoming aware of how close he is to me. I can feel the heat radiating from his body, and I find myself unintentionally drifting closer.

I must look like an idiot as I blink at him, attempting to unfreeze my brain. When I don't respond, he prompts, "Would that be okay?" He puts gentle pressure on my arm, sending another jolt of something unexpected through me.

Without another thought, I rip my arm away and scurry towards the kitchenette, trying my best to look professional as I do.

I barely have time to recover before Katina comes in, arms loaded with trays of salads. I don't envy her shift with the catering crew.

"Hey, we keep the extra bread baskets in here, right?" she asks, scanning the room.

"Yeah, why?"

"The hot groomsman asked for you to bring extra bread for the table," she says with a slight smirk. "Could you bring another basket out?"

I sigh, immediately knowing she's referring to Alex. I uncover a basket from the counter and hold it out to her.

"Here, I'll let you deliver bread to the 'hot groomsman.' You can leave the salads for half a minute without anyone losing their head," I tell her. Her face lights up, and she hurries off to the bridal party table.

I watch from the kitchenette, feeling satisfied, but only for a moment. Something burns low in my stomach as I think of Katina referring to Alex as hot. I'm not sure I like it.

Alex catches my eye just before I can duck back into the kitchenette. He's amused, which is a good look for him. He raises his eyebrows at me slightly, not breaking eye contact as Katina delivers the bread.

I manage to tear myself away from his gaze and focus instead on taking inventory of the boxes of extra cookies stacked high on the counters. It doesn't keep me busy for long, but it at least gets me through to the speeches, which are quickly followed by dinner. I do my best to tune out Alex's voice, but his words work their way into my brain as he mixes humor and sentiment almost perfectly.

I do my best to help my coworkers as they set up for the buffet-style dinner, but there are more than enough people taking care of it. Even the bartenders, who are almost always swamped, don't need any extra help.

I decide to head back over to the kitchenette, keeping my eyes ahead of me to avoid any more run-ins with Alex. Part of me wants to hear him out, but another part of me wants to push him down a flight of stairs. The rest of me is just confused.

I'm startled to find Alex waiting for me in the kitchenette.

"Would you happen to have extra silverware in here? I, uh, dropped mine." His boyish grin spreads, still the same after all these years.

I wordlessly open a drawer and retrieve a set of silverware, perfectly wrapped in a blue cloth napkin. I set it in his open hand, but I don't let go. We stay frozen in place, and I can't help but remember how it felt to hold his hand all those years ago. I wonder if it would still feel the same.

"You know, while we're in here, I'd really love to talk," he says after a long stretch of heavy silence.

"I'm not sure this is the right time or place." I gesture around the small, enclosed room.

"Name the time and place."

"Alex," I sigh. His eyes glimmer at me at the sound of his name. "Don't you have a wedding to get back to?"

He doesn't take his eyes off me, but I can tell that he's considering this. He starts to walk back toward his table, but just before he leaves, he abruptly turns and leans in close. His mouth is suddenly inches from my ear as he softly says, "I hope you know that I'm going to keep finding ways to talk to you until you agree to start listening."

"What if I don't want to listen?" I ask breathlessly.

He pulls back. "If you can look me in the eyes and tell me that there isn't a single ounce of you that wants to hear what I have to say, then I'll drop it."

When I don't respond, his smile returns. "See you on the dance floor."

The last hour has been less than eventful, thanks to dinner. Everyone takes their time eating, and the servers are all over the reception space. They handle the guests as dinner comes to an end while I pay a visit to Amber and catch her up on everything.

As I expected, she urges me to have some 'alone time' with him. My stomach does cartwheels at the thought.

"What're you even doing down here with me? You could be with your hunk of a man right now!" she squeals.

"He isn't my man." I defend.

"But he is a hunk," she counters, poking me with a pretzel stick, "And you want him to be yours."

"Maybe I did at one point." I concede.

"Ha!" She takes a triumphant bite of her pretzel.

"But that was a long time ago. I don't feel the same."

She rolls her eyes dramatically. "We both know there isn't much truth to that. Besides, he's clearly into you, and maybe he has a good explanation for everything that happened."

"You mean like in sitcoms where there is always a perfectly accept-able reason that the main character conveniently overlooks because they get too caught up in their feelings?"

"Exactly!"

Now it's my turn to roll my eyes. "Even with a good reason, I do not feel the same way about him."

"If you don't, then why are you telling me all of this?" she asks, swat-ting me with her dishrag. "Now, get back out there before all the servers go on break. Dinner should be about over."

Right on cue, Jacob walks into the dish room, holding an extra basket of bread and two plastic cups filled with something pink and bubbly. I chuckle as Amber pounces on him, and I can barely hear her say, "Oh my gosh! You're an angel," before the loud music coming from the reception drowns them out.

I must've been gone longer than I thought because the lighting has been drastically dimmed, and the guests are all dancing to an old throwback song. As expected, Alex is at the center of the dance circle with the groom. He's always been the life of the party.

I notice that the cookie table is severely lacking, so I take my time replenishing it. I'm just setting out the last of the cheesecake brownie bites when I see a flash of something out of the corner of my eye.

I turn to see Alex picking up a flaming blue cloth napkin from the table closest to me. His eyes are filled with panic and surprise.

I don't waste a second thinking. I hurry over to him, snatch the napkin, and rush over to the kitchenette. I throw it in the sink and immediately douse it in water. To my relief, it's nothing more than a charred napkin after about ten seconds. Still, I'm shaking, and my heart is threatening to thump right out of my chest. I could throw up.

"Okay, I know I said I'd keep getting you to come talk to me, but this one was an accident," Alex says from behind me. I turn to face him, surprised at how close he's standing.

"How the heck did that even happen?" I struggle to keep my voice steady.

"It's actually a funny story. I was coming over to talk to you under the guise of wanting some cookies, but I bumped the table when I was walking past it. The candle in the centerpiece toppled over onto the napkin, and the rest is history."

His voice comes out smooth, but he's visibly a little shaken up. I don't doubt his story for a second. I'm sure the last thing he would want to do is take away from the happy couple's big day with a small fire.

"Do you think anyone saw that?" My face burns with embarrassment as I look up at him, even though I know it wasn't my fault.

"I don't think so," he says. "I think we're good."

"I really hope that's true." My eyes dart nervously to the reception, which seems undisturbed.

I must look as worried as I feel. He reaches out to rub my arm, making my heartbeat faster for a whole new reason.

"I don't remember you being so keen on physical contact," I murmur.

He shrugs, and the corner of his mouth twitches up into a half-smile. "I guess I'm touchy when I'm with you. Is that . . . okay?"

My mouth has gone dry, so I manage a nod.

His smile grows. "I'm going to get back out there. Talk later?" I nod again, feeling a little dazed.

The next hour and a half go by in a blur as I focus on keeping up with the rapidly disappearing cookies, stealing glances at Alex, who is always looking, and wondering what the heck is wrong with me.

When I check my phone, I see a text from Amber telling me that it's finally time for our dinner break. My stomach rumbles at the thought of food, and I realize that I've hardly eaten anything in the last several hours aside from the occasional cookie.

Jacob is coming into the kitchenette just as I'm leaving. "Did Amber tell you to go eat?" he asks.

"Yup, I'm guessing you're going to be covering for me."

"Bingo."

"Have fun." I start to turn away, but at the last minute, I look back at him. "Snickerdoodles are Amber's favorite. They're in that white box." I gesture to the box perched on the counter to his left and give him a little wink as I hustle off to dinner.

Amber is already piling food onto her plate in the kitchen, and I waste no time grabbing my own plate. I load up on steak, potatoes, salad, and the extra appetizers sitting in the warmer.

Satisfied with the amount of food we're managing to balance, we head toward one of the outdoor tables on the lower deck. It's a perfect night to eat outside now that the sun has mostly gone down, and with all of the guests being upstairs, we get to enjoy it down below.

We take the first few bites in happy silence, appreciating the amazing food that our chefs never fail to produce. I make a mental note to ask for the recipe they used for the potatoes, which may be the most incredible thing I've ever tasted.

"So, how's your man?" Amber asks through a mouthful of steak.

I'm ready to give up on reasoning with her. "Not my man, but I think I might be going crazy because I'm actually considering talking to him."

"Oh, my goodness, finally! Even if you don't do it for yourself, do it for me." She bats her lashes sweetly.

"We'll see," I say, trying to find a subject change. Aha, got one. "Anyway, I'm much more concerned about *your* man," I tease.

She crinkles her nose at me. "My man?"

"Yup, Jacob."

I expect her to shoot down the notion immediately, but she just blushes and takes a sip from her cup.

"What about him?" she finally responds.

"Amber! It's obvious that he's into you, but I didn't think you liked him back!"

"I didn't think I did either, especially after how rude he used to be towards me. Do you remember how he would barely even talk to me back when I first started here?" she asks.

"I do, but that was a long time ago," I tell her. "People grow."

She raises her eyebrows at me, emphasizing the irony in my words. "People do grow," she agrees.

Maybe Alex has done some growing of his own.

It all happens so quickly that I don't have time to process whether or not it's a good idea, but I don't mind.

It started with Leonard asking me to help him move a few racks of glasses to the upper bar. Once we finished that up, I walked the perimeter of the dance floor to get back to the kitchenette.

A hand—a large, warm hand—wrapped around my wrist and tugged me into the swarm of people on the dance floor. The hand spun me around to face the body attached to it. Alex, to my relief.

An old song that used to top the pop music charts in high school was blasting through the speakers, and Alex was singing and dancing along. His movements were clumsy, and he was off pitch, but he looked like he was having a blast.

Without thinking, I started singing and dancing along with him. Of course, the song came to an end in a few minutes, and to my surprise, a slow song came on next. A love song. My favorite love song. One that I had only ever mentioned to Alex on one occasion several years ago.

I raised my eyebrows at him, and his eyes softened. There was no way this was a coincidence. His smile grew as he held out his hand to me, silently asking me to dance with him.

Now, here I am, swaying slowly in Alex's arms without a thought in my head—other than that this feels even better than it had five years ago.

His arms tighten around me with every passing minute. His heartbeat thumps against my cheek in a calming rhythm. His subtle cologne fills my lungs and puts me at ease. It is absolutely heavenly.

That is until I feel myself getting ripped away from his warmth right as the final notes of the song ring out. Slightly dazed, I look up to see Jacob, who is staring daggers at Alex.

"What's your deal, man?" Jacob yell-whispers at Alex, trying not to draw any attention. Jacob is fuming, while Alex looks as if something has been stolen from him.

"I'm sorry, I didn't think a few minutes would be a big deal," Alex whispers back.

"Any amount of time is a big deal when you're harassing someone!" Jacob barely keeps himself contained. Realization dawns on Alex's face.

"Oh, no, that's not what happened. We know each other," he shifts his gaze to me.

Realizing I've been silent this whole time, I step in. "He's right, Jacob. We're old friends, and I agreed to dance with him."

Jacob gives Alex a final glare before pulling me away to the kitchenette.

"Are you sure nothing else happened? You can tell me now that it's just us," Jacob says once we're in the tiny room.

"I promise, I agreed to dance with him. He didn't do anything wrong," I assure him.

After a second, his features relax. "Okay, that's a relief."

"Thanks for looking out for me," I offer him a smile and pat his shoulder. "I really appreciate it."

"Of course, I wouldn't want anything bad to happen to you. After all, that means we'd have one less person to help close tonight, and nobody else can fold tablecloths as well as you." He cracks a smile and gently pats the top of my head before leaving.

Feeling embarrassed, I spend the last hour or so of the night avoiding Alex. Unlike my attempts earlier in the day, this one is successful. It isn't until the reception ends and we start closing that I see him again. Even then, it starts as nothing more than brief eye contact from across the room as we both work to organize everything and clean up.

He watches me carry one of the three massive coffee urns from the little coffee station on the top deck to the kitchenette, and when I go back for another, he's already there. Wordlessly, we each grab an urn and take it to the kitchenette.

"I'm going to stick around as long as they'll have me, and after, I'll be at the gazebo. I hope you'll join me when you finish up," he says. He gives me a hopeful smile before returning to the reception space, where the bridesmaids and groomsmen are collecting the centerpieces and other decorations they brought.

I realize that I no longer feel skeptical when I think of hearing him out, and suddenly, the end of this shift can't come fast enough.

Despite my resurgence of feelings for him, I'm still nervous as I walk through the yard over an hour later.

I'm sweaty and exhausted, and I look like a mess, but I light up when I see Alex. Even in the darkness, I can see him light up, too.

"I'm so happy to see you," he beams. "Actually, I've been happy to see you all day. And I've been wanting to tell you something all day, too."

I nod, smiling and eager to listen despite my apprehension.

"I know I hurt you before, and I'm not going to make any excuses. I messed up. I made the wrong decision that night, and I've always regretted it. I know I can't take it back, even though I'm sure we both wish I could, but I am so sorry."

I hate to think of what happened, but I let myself go back to how I felt all those years ago. I picture him locking lips with my best friend, throwing away the plans he made with me. Even though I can still feel the pain as if it all happened just a moment ago, that pales in comparison to how my heart soars now as I look into his eyes.

"I've grown a lot in the last few years, and I want to show you how I can be better," he tells me. My heart feels as if it's been pumped so full that it's seconds away from bursting.

His eyes anxiously search mine as he waits for me to respond.

"I think we've both grown," I tell him with a smile, pushing away my reservations towards him. "I'd like to find out how."

Relief takes over his face as he pulls me into his arms for the second time today. "That. Sounds. Perfect," he punctuates each word with a kiss on my forehead.

"Oh, baby! Get it!" I recognize Amber's voice shouting at us, and we turn in the direction of the barn to see her waving. She whistles loudly before letting out a final yell, "That's my girl."

Alex's body shakes with laughter against mine, and though I feel my face get red, I'm so grateful for Amber. From a distance, I watch Jacob walk up beside her. He leans in to say something to her, and I might be imagining it, but I swear I see him take her hand.

Seeing the two of them warms my heart, but when Alex gently turns my face back to his and lowers his mouth to meet mine, my heart catches on fire, and I melt into him.

Reading Questions

1. From ceremonies to guest experiences, wedding rituals and expectations vary by culture and time. How did the events in this anthology compare to your encounters at weddings?

2. The Charged Encounters section features various depictions of or allusions to illegal or morally questionable behavior. Discuss how such behavior functions as a metaphor amidst the backdrop of a wedding.

3. Consider why the "Rocketship Derivative" narrator mentions Hemingway four times. How does the story parallel, intersect, or deviate from Hemingway's exploration of relationships and marriage?

4. What do petunias symbolize? Explore how their presence in "Petunias and Parenting at the Wedding" can enhance character analysis.

5. Would you have had any characters make different decisions? Explain.

M uñeca Fossette (a faux alias) inadvertently exists in contradiction. She is a socially introverted, polyglot, humanitarian, animal-loving educator who uses multiple languages to avoid engaging with humans. She lives a vegan lifestyle with her three omnivorous dogs and regularly receives visits from nomadic cats and larcenous raccoons.

More books from 4 Horsemen Publications

Romance

Ann Shepphird
The War Council

Emily Bunney
All or Nothing
All the Way
All Night Long: Novella
All She Needs
Having it All
All at Once
All Together
All for Her

KT Bond
Back to Life
Back to Love
Back at Last

Lynn Chantale
The Baker's Touch
Blind Secrets
Broken Lens
Blind Fury
Time Bomb

VIP's Revenge
Chef's Taste

Mandy Fate
Love Me, Goaltender
Captain of My Heart

Mimi Francis
Private Lives
Private Protection
Private Party
Run Away Home
The Professor
Our Two-Week, One-Night Stand

Shae Coon
Bound in Love
Controlling Assets
For His Own Protection
Her Broken Pieces
The Roma's Claim
The Roma's Promise

LGBT Romance

Eskay Kabba
Hidden Love
Not So Hidden
Signs of Affection

Lucas LaMont
Roman's Reckoning: Type 6
Mikaél's Moment: Type 6
Stephan's Resurgence: Type 5
Anastasia's Arrival: Type 6

Stormie Skyes
Check Yes, No, or Maybe

Anthologies & Collections

4HP Anthologies
Teen Angst: Mix Vol. 1
Teen Angst: Mix Vol. 2
My Wedding Date
The Offices of Supernatural Being
The Sentient Space

Demonic Anthologies
Demonic Wildlife
Demonic Household
Demonic Carnival
Demonic Classics
Demonic Vacations
Demonic Medicine
Demonic Workplace
& more to follow!

Discover more at
4HorsemenPublications.com